"Am I supposed to live like a monk just because I have a kid in the house?" Nick asked.

Lily didn't know how to answer. Maybe he should ask one of the other moms in the neighborhood— ones who had more active social lives. Except Lily didn't want him anywhere near other women.

"I don't know if I'm the person to ask about this," Lily said. "I mean, I guess you could hope to find a woman with no kids and a place of her own and make an early night of it. So your nephew isn't home alone for long."

Nick looked at her, a wide grin on his face. "Not gonna work. The woman I've got my eye on has two little girls."

"Oh." Lily nearly dropped her glass.

Nick saved her by taking it out of her hand and putting it down. Then he took her chin in his hand and very slowly, giving her time to pull away if she wanted to, leaned in close, his nose nuzzling hers, lips practically on hers.

"It's you, Lily. The woman I want is you."

Dear Reader,

People often ask how much of ourselves and the people around us we put into our books. I usually say bits and pieces of my life and many other people's lives.

Still, I'd be lying if I said that, as a mother, I didn't particularly enjoy some of the dialogue in this book.

Especially when poor Nick, baffled by the world of parenting and sometimes terrified by it, says something like, "Teenagers? Are they just stupid or what? I mean, I've seen the kid's report card. I know he's not stupid!"

Or Jake, out too late at night, knowing he shouldn't be and not answering the frantic calls to his cell phone, then explaining later, "Well, I knew you'd be mad, and I didn't know what to say. So I just didn't answer the phone."

Right. Makes perfect sense. We've all been there and heard that, haven't we?

I should say in my own kids' defense that so far, neither one has wrecked a car and that we haven't been to the emergency room since our son was six weeks old and had an ear infection. (Thank God.) Still, it's a big, scary world raising kids, especially teenagers.

Here's wishing yours are all safe, smart and home by curfew.

Teresa Hill

SINGLE MOM SEEKS...

TERESA HILL

SPECIAL EDITION

Published by Silhouette Books

America's Publisher of Contemporary Romance

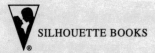

SILHOUETTE BOOKS

Recycling programs
for this product may
not exist in your area.

ISBN-13: 978-0-373-65431-4
ISBN-10:   0-373-65431-6

SINGLE MOM SEEKS...

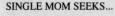

Visit Silhouette Books at www.eHarlequin.com

Printed in U.S.A.

Books by Teresa Hill

Silhouette Special Edition

Heard It Through the Grapevine #1546
A Little Bit Engaged #1740
Her Sister's Fiancé #1793
Mr. Right Next Door #1829
Single Mom Seeks... #1949

TERESA HILL

lives within sight of the mountains in upstate South Carolina with one husband, very understanding and supportive; one daughter, who's taken up drumming (Earplugs really don't work that well. Neither do sound-muffling drum pads. Don't believe anyone who says they do.); and one son, who's studying the completely incomprehensible subject of chemical engineering. (Flow rates, Mom. It's all about flow rates.)

In search of company while she writes away her days in her office, she has so far accumulated two beautiful, spoiled dogs and three cats (the black panther/champion hunter, the giant powder puff and the tiny tiger stripe), all of whom take turns being stretched out, belly-up on the floor beside her, begging for attention as she sits at her computer.

To all mothers who've survived raising teenagers.
You have my complete admiration.

Chapter One

"I just don't see what all the fuss is about," Lily Tanner told her older sister, Marcy, as she scrambled to hold the phone to her ear with her shoulder while making sandwiches for her two girls' school lunches.

"Fuss?" Her sister seemed disbelieving. "That's what you call it? Fuss?"

"No, I don't call it fuss," Lily said, smearing peanut butter on the bread too fast and tearing a gash in the last slice she had, save for the heels. Her girls acted like she was trying to feed them some kind of brick when she had nothing but the heels of a loaf of bread to offer.

"Who's fussing?" her youngest, Brittany, who was six, asked.

"No one's fussing," Lily assured her, as her daughter moved like a sloth through the kitchen, slowly sipping a cup of milk, like she had all the time in the world before Tuesday's designated carpool driver arrived.

"And no one's getting any fuss," Marcy told her. "Which is

fine for a while and completely understandable, given what that rat Richard put you through. But after a while, a woman's just got to have a little fussing."

"Oh, for God's sake, I am not going to call it fussing," Lily said, trying to salvage the torn slice of bread. Anything but the heel. She wasn't taking lip from her daughters today about a heel of bread in a peanut butter sandwich.

"You said nobody was fussing," Brittany reminded her.

"Fussing? Who's fussing?" her oldest, Ginny, asked, looking worried, as she too often did these days. "Is it Daddy? Are you and Daddy fussing?"

"No. I told you. No one's fussing," Lily promised, rolling her eyes in exasperation. "Your aunt Marcy and I were just talking, and we weren't actually talking about fussing at all. We were talking about—"

"Yes, please. I can't wait to hear," Marcy said, laughing. "Tell me what we were talking about."

"Fudge," Lily said, thinking it was the farthest thing from fussing she could come up with on short notice.

Marcy roared at that.

Lily shoved sandwiches into lunch boxes as Ginny looked like she didn't quite believe her own mother.

Then Brittany piped up and saved the day, announcing with absolute sincerity, an unwavering sense of optimism and six-year-old innocence, "I like fudge."

"There," Lily said, managing a smile for her girls. "Everybody likes fudge."

"Everybody certainly does," Marcy said. "So for you to tell me that you're perfectly fine without—"

"Marcy!" she yelled into the phone while she shooed the girls toward the front door.

"Wait," Brittany said, stopping short and tugging on the right leg of Lily's shorts. "Do we have fudge?"

"No, baby. Not right now. But maybe tonight," Lily said.

"Here. I've got the front door. You two have to get outside. Mrs. Hamilton will be here any minute."

She hustled the girls out the door, waved to Betsy Hamilton, who was already at the curb, then closed the door and turned her attention back to the phone.

"Honestly, Marcy! Fudge?"

"Hey, it was your word, not mine. But now that you've coined the term, we're stuck with it. It's perfect. It'll be our code word forever."

"We don't need a code word. We don't need to talk about it at all. I am perfectly fine," Lily insisted.

After all, it was just…fudge. Nothing to get all that excited about. Not when she had fifteen things to do every minute of the day and the girls ran her ragged and Richard was still as annoying as could be.

Who had time for fudge?

"May I remind you," Lily said, "that I have a year to get out of this house? Not even that, anymore. Just a little over ten and a half months to do everything I can to upgrade it before I have to sell it and hope I get enough out of my half to get me and the girls into another house. Which is going to take every bit of time and energy I have for the next ten and a half months."

"I know. I know."

"And where am I supposed to find a man anyway? You know what it's like in my neighborhood. Everybody's married, with kids the girls' ages, and if they do happen to get divorced, the wife ends up here in the subdivision with the kids while the cheating husband moves out to some little love nest of an apartment with his new, pretty, young thing. Until the wife has to sell out for lack of money and then some new married couple moves in. These are the suburbs, in all their glory. I could easily go a month without seeing a single, eligible man, and then even if one did show up, I don't have time to date anybody. I hardly have time to drink my coffee."

She gave a big huff at the end of her little speech, tired and spent.

Did her sister know nothing of Lily's current life? Of her world?

It was maddening and annoying and more than a little sad to feel so alone and to be living in such aggravating circumstances, just because Richard met a girl barely out of her teens on a business trip to Baltimore.

"Oh, honey. I'm sorry," Marcy said, and Lily could hear Marcy's own kids in the background now. "I wasn't trying to make things harder for you. I was just trying to warn you that it's fine to go without…fudge for a while, and then…well, then it's not. I mean, you're still human, and you're only thirty-four years old. We all have needs. We all get lonely."

"I am not lonely," Lily insisted, clearing the table of half-eaten bowls of cereal and bread crumbs from the peanut butter sandwiches and half-empty glasses that seemed to multiply like rabbits all over the house when Lily's back was turned. "At least not for…fudge. Now, a bubble bath, I could handle. Someone to cook dinner every now and then or a good book, plus enough time to read it without interruptions—that I could handle. But fudge is—"

Lily broke off as she straightened up, having put four cups in the dishwasher and found herself looking out the window above the sink, which faced the house next door, which had been empty for weeks.

It looked like it wasn't going to be empty anymore, because in the driveway was a moving truck backed up to the garage, the big back door of the truck open, a pair of sun-bronzed, muscular arms handing a table out of the back of the truck to someone Lily couldn't quite see because of an overgrown rhododendron bush.

"What?" Marcy asked. "Where did you go?"

"Right here," Lily said, watching as the arms kept coming out, soon to be followed by a really nice, perfectly muscled shoulder.

First one.

Then the other.

Lily was afraid her mouth dropped open, and she just couldn't seem to shut it.

Legs. Long, masculine legs, encased in well-worn jeans that hung just a tad low on a taut waist, above which was what looked to be the most beautifully formed washboard abs she'd ever seen, and above that, nice, broad, extremely capable looking shoulders.

"Oh," Lily said, all the breath going out of her in a rush.

"What?" Marcy asked. "Are you okay?"

Lily felt like she'd been burned.

A wave of heat came over her, blossoming in the pit of her stomach and spreading like a flood to every cell in her body.

There was an absolutely gorgeous male creature at the house next door, muscles flexing beautifully, a little sweat on his brow, chest gloriously naked, and all of a sudden she got it. Everything her sister had been trying to explain to her about loneliness and needs and how some things were fine for a while and then, they just weren't anymore.

Suddenly, they were urgent, burning, overwhelming.

"Oh, fudge!" Lily said and dropped the phone.

She was afraid he'd seen her watching him through the kitchen window or that somehow he'd heard her phone clattering on the hard tile floor. Which seemed impossible at this distance and with the walls of her house between them.

But his head shot around and he stared right at her before she gulped and dropped to her knees, feeling guilty and confused and hot all over.

Like she'd suddenly developed a fever in mere seconds.

Maybe she was coming down with something.

Lily touched her hand to her forehead to see if it felt hot.

A mother could tell those things just by the touch of her hand, after dealing with as many feverish kids as she had.

But she couldn't tell this time. Not for sure.

Rattled, she stood back up and looked cautiously out the window once again, to see nothing but the open back of the moving truck and a few boxes.

No sign of *him.*

Had to be one of the movers, she told herself as she searched the cabinet above the stove, where she stored medicines to keep out of her girls' reach.

Men in her neighborhood did not look that good without their shirts on. They didn't have those kinds of muscles or those kinds of tans.

They were strictly suit-and-tie kind of guys.

Desk jockeys.

Pencil pushers.

A man didn't get muscles like that in corporate America.

Lily found the thermometer and put it in her mouth, just as her phone rang stridently.

She must have dropped the phone just right to disconnect the call as it landed.

Which meant this had to be her sister calling back.

And Lily didn't want to talk to Marcy.

Not that Marcy would really give her the option of refusing. She'd just keep calling until Lily answered. Either that or get in her car and drive the twenty minutes between their houses to make sure Lily was okay.

Marcy tended to be a tad overprotective since Richard had moved out.

"Oh, fine," she muttered, picking up the phone, thermometer still in her mouth. "Hewwo."

"What happened?" Marcy demanded to know.

"Sowwy. I dwopped d'phone," Lily said as best she could. "Huh?"

"Wait...." The thermometer beeped and she took it out. No

fever. How odd. "I was just taking my temperature. I felt a little warm, and I dropped the phone."

Not necessarily in that order, but Marcy didn't have to know every little thing.

"You think you have a fever? From just talking about... fudge?"

Lily rolled her eyes. Marcy's kids must still be there. They left for school about fifteen minutes later than Lily's.

"No, not from just talking about it. I just felt...warm, that's all."

"You're not telling me something," Marcy insisted.

"There's a lot I don't tell you or anyone else," Lily admitted, leaning every so slightly to the left, so she could see out the kitchen window again.

And there he was, unloading a kitchen chair.

Lily sighed heavily, unable to help herself.

"I knew it!" Marcy pounced on the sound. "What's going on? Do you have a man there?"

"No, I do not have a man here, and I don't want a man here. I just got rid of one, and he was enough trouble to last me a lifetime," she insisted.

"Honey, we just talked about this. You are not off men for a lifetime. You think you are, but I promise you, you're not. You're just in deep freeze right now."

"Deep freeze?"

"Yes. Where men are concerned. But you won't always be there. One day, some man will come along and bam! No more deep freeze on your...fudge life."

"Aunt Lily has a fudge life?" she heard Marcy's youngest ask through the phone.

Lily started laughing.

"What's a fudge life?" Stacy asked. "Do you just eat it and eat it and eat it all day?"

"No," Marcy insisted.

"'Cause I like fudge. Could I have a fudge life?"

"No. No one spends her life eating fudge," Marcy said, then hissed at her sister, "Fudge life? I will never hear the end of this. She'll probably tell the other kids at school, and I'll be getting calls from the other moms. All their kids will want a fudge life, and the moms will want to know what I'm doing, telling kids they can just eat fudge all the time. How am I ever going to explain this?"

"Sorry. Gotta go," Lily said, hearing her sister growl at her before she hung up the phone.

A fudge life?

Lily laughed again.

At least she could do that now. Laugh at times.

She hadn't for a while. It had been too hard, too scary, too overwhelming, to think of being mostly alone in the world except for two little girls depending on her for just about everything.

But it was getting less overwhelming as time went on.

She was down, but she wasn't beaten.

Lily peeked out the window again, and he was still there, a big box perched on one shoulder, the muscles in his arm looking long and sleek and glistening with sweat.

Had to be a mover, she reassured herself.

Something looking that good would never move in next door to her.

And it was getting hot out.

They probably didn't have anything cold to drink in that house, which had been empty for three months, since the Sanders got transferred to San Diego.

It would be neighborly to drop by and offer them a little something, and maybe the owners would show up while she was there. Or she could pump the moving men for information on the new family.

Her girls were always eager to have more friends to play with. The first thing they'd ask when they walked in the door after school would be whether the new neighbors had girls their age, and a good mother should be ready to provide the answers for her children, shouldn't she?

Lily opened the refrigerator door, thinking…a pitcher of iced tea?

Yes, she had one, very nearly full.

And some cookies?

She checked the cabinets. No cookie mix. Lily dug a little deeper, then sucked in a breath, feeling uneasy once again.

No, she didn't have any cookie mix.

But she had what she needed to make a batch of fudge.

Neighborly, she muttered to herself, as she marched across the yard with the pitcher of tea, four plastic glasses tucked under her arm, and a batch of still-warm fudge.

Just be *neighborly.*

Nothing more. Nothing less.

She made it to the back of the truck and could hear someone swearing softly from inside the enclosed space, and when she paused right behind the truck and looked in, she found him, eyes narrowed in concentration, right shoulder pressed up against a huge box that had snagged on the corner of another one and then didn't want to budge.

Up close, in his face she saw a toughness and a certain strength, eyes so dark they were almost black and flashing with irritation at the moment. He had an ultra-firm jaw, a head full of thick, dark brown hair that he wore a little too long, and what seemed like miles and miles of bare, brown skin.

It was all that skin and muscles that did it to her.

She started to feel hot all over again and thought about cooling her forehead with the tea pitcher, which was already sweating with condensation from the heat.

She'd be taking her temperature again when she got home, just to make sure. Because something wasn't right here.

"Hi. Can I help you, ma'am?" a deep voice said from behind her.

"Oh!" She startled, nearly spilling the tea before the nearly grown teenager, all arms and legs and hair, grabbed it and saved it.

"Jake!" the man who had made her feverish called out from behind her.

"Sorry," the kid, Jake, said. "Didn't mean to sneak up on you."

"Oh. No. It's all right. I just...didn't hear you." *I was too busy becoming feverish, possibly over your father.*

How embarrassing.

Did the kid know women reacted this way to his father?

Did his gorgeous dad know?

Lily wanted to sink into the rhododendron behind her.

"It's okay." The kid pointed to the plate of hot fudge in her hand. "Is that for us?"

"Jake!" The man, standing at the edge of the truck bed and looking down at them both, made the name sound like an order, not to be ignored.

A mind-your-manners-or-else order.

Lily glanced up at him nervously, then quickly looked away. Tall, hot, all muscles and no smile, she saw in a flash.

"Sorry." The kid looked properly apologetic. "I just... It's hot, and we've been at this for hours, and I'm hungry."

"You're always hungry," the man said, command still evident in the voice.

"Yes," Lily said, jumping in to save the boy. "I have nephews who are about your age. I know teenage boys are always hungry, and I thought I'd come over and...introduce myself."

"Sweet," Jake said, sounding truly appreciative as she held out the plate to him. "Jake Elliott. This is my uncle, Nick Malone."

Uncle.

Not *dad.*

Did they have a moving company together? Or maybe Jake and his family were moving in, and Uncle Nick was just helping out?

"I'm Lily Tanner, from next door." She nodded toward her house, then held up the pitcher. "Would you like some sweet tea?"

"Oh, yeah," Jake said, his mouth already full of fudge. "Hey, it's still all warm and gooey. Did you just make this?"

"Yes," Lily said.

"Sweet!"

Which she knew was his generation's current equivalent of *cool*.

"I bet she was thinking the fudge might make a good snack for later on," his uncle pointed out. "And before you stick any more of it in your mouth, you could say thank-you."

"Thanks," Jake muttered with a mouth full of fudge. "Really, ma'am. It's great."

"You're welcome." She offered him a plastic cup and then filled it with tea.

Lily braced herself to face Uncle Nick, who'd just jumped down out of the truck bed and onto the ground, landing just a tad too close for her own comfort.

He immediately grabbed a worn, white T-shirt from the truck bed and pulled it on in what Lily could only describe as a truly impressive rippling, flexing mix of muscles in his arms and chest.

She appreciated that, she told herself, he would cover up that way. And she'd have thought maybe her mysterious fever would have gone away, once he was more covered up. But no, it hadn't.

If anything, it was even hotter now that he was closer and staring at her with those intense, dark eyes of his and a jaw like granite.

"Sorry," he said. "I feel like I've told him a million times already to say please and thank-you, and it just never seems to sink in."

"I know. It's the same thing with my girls."

"You have girls?" Jake piped up at that.

Lily smiled at him. "Much too young for you, I'm afraid."

"I'm only fifteen," he said.

Which had to be impossible, it seemed. He was positively overgrown, this big, awkward, hulking thing who towered over her. The only thing boyish about him was his face.

"I know. I just look older," Jake said.

"You do. But my girls are only six and nine."

"Oh." He shrugged, like it was no big deal.

Lily was sure he had more girls than he could handle flirting with him, just like they must flirt with his uncle.

"I'm gonna go inside. Get out of the sun for a minute," Jake said, turning to leave. "Thanks again, Mrs. Tanner. This is great."

"You're welcome," Lily said, then found herself completely tongue-tied.

Flustered.

Flushed, she feared.

Feeling foolish.

She held out a cup to Mr. Tough-and-Sweaty, thinking sweat had surely never looked so good as it did on him.

"Thank you," he said, taking the cup and holding it out for her to fill, then shook his head. "That little rat escaped with all the fudge, didn't he?"

Lily smiled, not too big a smile, she hoped. Not like she was trying to flirt or anything. "I think he did. You should probably hurry inside. If he's anything like my nephews, he could down the whole plate easily inside of five minutes."

"Sounds like Jake," he agreed, tipping his head back as he took a long swallow of tea. "Wow, that's good."

"You're welcome to keep the pitcher," she offered. "I thought your refrigerator must be empty, and it's supposed to be in the nineties today, so... I just thought this was a good idea."

"It was. Jake and I appreciate it."

"So…are you moving in? Or is Jake and his family?" She hoped she sounded neighborly and nothing more, and that the flush on her face didn't give her away.

"Just Jake and me," he said, his expression if possible becoming even more stern. "My sister and her husband died in a car accident six weeks ago. They have twin boys in college at Virginia Commonwealth. Jake's their youngest. Other than the twins, I'm what passes for his family now."

"Oh. I'm so sorry," she said.

And here she had been admiring every bit of him, right down to the sweat on his brow. Admiring the sweat of a grieving man with a grieving teenage boy.

"Thanks. It's still a little raw, but—"

"Of course. I'm sorry I even asked—"

"No. I'm glad you did. Glad you asked me and not him. He's…uh…well, it still throws him, getting the question and not knowing what to say."

"Of course. My girls were the same way when my husband and I divorced. I mean, I know it's not the same thing, but…they hated having everyone ask, and then having to explain about their father not living with us anymore."

He nodded, quiet and understanding.

The kind of man who'd take on raising his fifteen-year-old nephew alone.

Which, if possible, only made him even more attractive. Maybe that stern expression was simply a result of what he'd been through in the last six weeks.

"Well, I should let you two get back to work," she said, handing him the pitcher. "Let me know if you need anything else. I'm almost always at home."

"Thanks again. This was really nice of you," he said quietly.

Nice.

Fine.

He thought she was nice.

She hoped he didn't know she was gawking like a smitten teenager over him, all while he was grieving for the loss of his sister and brother-in-law and taking care of his poor parentless nephew.

What is wrong with you? Lily muttered to herself, trying to hide her dismay behind a forced smile.

He nodded toward the house. "I'm going to get inside and have some of that fudge."

Yeah. She nodded goodbye.

Fudge.

Chapter Two

Jake was shoving fudge into his mouth like there was no tomorrow when Nick finally got into the kitchen of their new house. He stopped only long enough to hold out his now empty glass, wanting Nick to refill it for him before putting the pitcher down on the counter.

"Hey, she was kind of cute for somebody's mom," Jake said. "And she can really make fudge."

"I wouldn't know. I haven't had any yet," Nick said, hoping his voice wasn't too gruff.

He didn't mean for it to be. Too many years of snapping out orders to soldiers in his command. It was habit now, though he tried his best to tone it down for Jake and his brothers. They really didn't need anybody who sounded like they were yelling at them or mad at them, and Nick knew he could sound like that without even trying.

Jake handed over what was left of the fudge and Nick bit into it, a flavor akin to ecstasy exploding in his mouth.

"Oh…sh…man!" he said.

He was trying to quit cussing, too, trying to set a good example for the kid. Not that he was doing all that well with the no-swearing bit, either.

"I know," Jake said appreciatively. "What do you think we'd have to do to get her to make us dinner?"

"Doubtful. She's a single mother with two little girls," Nick said, still savoring a mouthful of fudge. "She probably doesn't have a lot of extra time."

"Still," Jake said hopefully. "I bet she'd do it for you. Did you see the way she looked at you? Like she didn't really mind that you're—"

"Old?" Nick guessed.

"I was going to say practically ancient." Jake grinned, reaching for the last piece of fudge.

"Touch it and die," Nick growled. "You already had a plateful."

"I know, but I'm still hungry," he complained.

And it wasn't even ten o'clock.

Lily Tanner knew what she was talking about. Teenage boys were bottomless pits. Nick hadn't noticed so much in the first week or so after his sister and brother-in-law's death, because neighbors kept bringing over food. It seemed like a mountain of food, but it hadn't lasted long with the twins and Jake in the house. It seemed nothing, even grief, dimmed the appetite of a teenage boy for long.

"Let's finish getting everything out of the truck before it gets any hotter, and then we'll go find something to eat," Nick said. "Who knows? Maybe by that time, another one of the neighbors will show up with lunch. Just try to look pitiful and weak and underfed."

"I can do that," Jake said, guzzling another glass of tea and then heading outside.

Nick put down his own glass, grabbed the last piece of fudge and popped it in his mouth, then looked around the house, empty of everything but boxes and furniture that hadn't yet been put into place, and he hoped for what had to be the thousandth time that he was doing the right thing in coming here to Virginia and trying to raise this kid.

And wondered what in the hell his sister had been thinking of to name him the boys' guardian in her will.

They got everything out of the truck by noon, and then went inside and moved just enough boxes to allow them room to collapse on the sofa that had landed temporarily right under a ceiling fan.

Nick had to hand it to the kid. He could do some work, and he was really strong, although Nick had to think he could take the kid in a fight, if he really had to. And from the mountain of unsolicited advice he'd received in the last few weeks on raising teenagers, Nick had been led to believe it might just come down to who was stronger physically at least once. Although, he couldn't see Jake refusing to listen to him to the point where the two of them got into a fight.

Still, what did Nick know? Next to nothing about raising kids.

Thank God they were boys.

If they had been girls, he wouldn't have had a prayer.

Of course, if his sister had daughters, she probably wouldn't have left them to Nick to raise.

"I'm starving," Jake said, sprawled out on the couch, eyes closed, head resting heavily against the back, long legs stretched out in front of him.

"Tell me something I don't already know," Nick said, thinking of what kind of fast-food restaurants he'd seen on the drive over here in the truck.

And then, the doorbell rang.

Jake sat up and looked insanely hopeful. "Do you think it might be more fudge?"

"I think we could use something more substantial than fudge. Don't you?"

"Guess so," Jake said, dragging himself up to answer the door.

Which was a good thing, because every muscle in Nick's body was protesting the very idea of moving, which the kid would no doubt give him hell about.

Nick didn't want to be fifteen again for any amount of money in the world, but the body of a fifteen-year-old... That, he could handle, especially on days like today.

Jake opened the door and grinned like crazy.

Must be food.

Nick forced himself up and to his feet, trying to make it without a grimace as his back protested fiercely. At least the kid didn't see. He was focused completely on the baking dish placed in his outstretched hands.

They made nice to the neighbor lady with the chicken cheddar noodle dish for a few minutes, then headed for the kitchen and scarfed it down right out of the pan, leaning over the kitchen countertop with a fork for each of them and nothing else.

Jake's mother would be appalled, Nick was sure, but hey, the kid was hungry and he was being fed.

They washed it down with some more of Lily Tanner's tea, Jake all but licking the chicken pan clean, like a puppy who hadn't been fed in days.

"I think I like this neighborhood," he said. "Do you think someone will show up with dinner?"

"We can hope," Nick said.

Lily had meant to get some work done that day. Truly, she had. She'd come home from next door and taken her temperature again, finding it still oddly normal, but still felt all flushed and shaky and...weak.

Was she coming down with something?

Had to be, she decided.

What other explanation could there be?

And then she went to work in her dining room, where the

walls were nothing but Sheetrock, ready for taping and spack-ling, then wallpaper, paint and wood trim.

She'd been an interior decorator before the girls were born, then a stay-at-home mom and then kind of fallen into the whole rehabbing thing. She'd convinced Richard they should sell their smaller house and buy a larger one in need of remodeling three years ago and hadn't looked back since.

A year there and a lot of work, mostly on Lily's part, which she found she truly enjoyed, and they'd sold the house at a nice profit and bought another one.

This was their fourth, bought just weeks before Richard an-nounced he was leaving her, and as part of the divorce settle-ment, she owed him half the equity they had in the house when they'd first purchased it. But she had a full year in which to finish renovating it and she got to keep everything she got over the original purchase price.

She'd worked hard to get that agreement and was counting on the profits from the house to allow her to outright buy a much smaller house for her and the girls to live in.

So she did not lack work to do that day, but the phone never stopped ringing. It seemed half the neighbors in the cul-de-sac had seen her talking to that gorgeous specimen of man next door and wanted to know a) If he was really moving in, b) If the teenager was his son, and c) If the gorgeous man could possibly be single.

Having all the answers to all three questions, Lily was a very popular woman that morning. Not to be outdone by a gift of fudge and iced tea, her neighbors promptly went to work.

By noon, there was a veritable parade of women marching to the house next door, casserole dishes in hand, bright smiles on what looked to Lily like perfectly made-up faces and clothes more suited for a fancy lunch out than a casual drop-in on a new neighbor.

"Shameless," Lily muttered to herself, again at that kitchen window, watching Jean Sumner from three doors down show up in a low-cut sweater that hugged her more than ample curves. "Absolutely shameless."

Her new neighbors would enjoy the view much more than what Lily would bet was Jean's curried turkey, which Lily knew from experience tended to be quite dry.

Sissy Williams just happened to drop by in her little white tennis outfit, practically bouncing in enthusiasm as she presented them with what looked like a cake.

Jake would like that.

But the most shameless one of all, as far as Lily was concerned, was Audrey Graham, showing up at their front door in jogging shorts and a jog bra!

"You could at least put a shirt on!" Lily muttered, knowing good and well the woman couldn't hear her.

At least Lily had shown up with all her clothes on, and she hadn't dressed up. She felt vastly superior to the parade of neighbors she'd seen so far just because she hadn't fussed over her appearance or shown an excessive amount of skin.

She wondered if her neighbors, too, had felt a little feverish after their visits, because Nick's shirt had come back off while he was unloading the truck. Lily couldn't help but notice, being right next door and all.

But she hadn't gawked at him or anything like that. It was just that in passing by her kitchen window, which she did on a regular basis on any given day, she happened to glance out and there he was, him and Jake and a parade of food-bearing, scantily clad women.

Lily had never known her neighbors to behave in this way. This was a very respectable street, in a well-respected neighborhood, after all.

Lily's sister called again, but Lily got away with being remarkably vague about her day, and there was no more talk about fudge of any kind. The girls came home from school, happy and full of energy until after she fed them and mentioned homework. At which point, they pled an overwhelming case of fatigue and collapsed on the floor of the family room, watching a Disney Channel movie until she shooed them off to bed at eight-thirty.

Lily was loading the dishwasher a few minutes later when she caught sight of Jake cutting through the side yard and heading for her kitchen door.

She didn't fuss. Not really.

Patted down her hair, checked her shirt to make sure she wasn't dusty or really dirty, because she had gotten a little work in on prepping the dining-room walls that day, and then she pulled open the door.

Jake stood there about to knock, looking like a giant puppy, all hair and ears and feet.

"Hi. Get everything moved in?"

"Yes, ma'am," he said, coming inside.

"You must be tired," she said.

"A little," he admitted, like it would take more than a day like this to make a boy his age actually tired.

"What can I do for you?" she offered.

"Well…I kind of messed up, and I'm not sure what to do about it," he confessed. "See, we had all these people come over and bring food. All kinds of good food—"

"Yes. I noticed," Lily admitted.

"Nothing as good as your fudge. But good stuff, and my uncle told me to keep a list of who brought what and what it was in, so we could get the plates and pans back to everybody and thank them, and I…well, I kind of have a list, but…not really."

"Ah." Lily nodded. "You got hungry and got distracted and…"

"Yeah. I did. And now, I'm not sure what to do. I have cards and things with names on them, but they're not all attached to dishes anymore, and I think I remember what some of the women looked like who brought certain things…."

Like Audrey in the jog bra.

Lily bet Jake remembered her.

"I can probably match up most of the dishes to the cards," Lily assured him. "We tend to bring over the same recipes when we do meals for people. I know everyone's specialties."

He looked so grateful she wanted to hug him.

Poor baby.

He must have had a long day and a really bad six weeks or so.

"Look, my girls are upstairs asleep—"

"I could stay here, in case they wake up," he offered.

"Okay," Lily said. "It won't take me a minute. Everything's in the refrigerator?"

He nodded. "And the cards and stuff are on the counter by the refrigerator. I left the side door open, and my uncle went to drive the truck back to the rental place, so the house is empty."

"Okay. Be right back."

She knew the house from when the last couple lived there, and her kitchen faced theirs, so all she had to do was get around the low row of bushes and she was there. And everything was right where Jake said it would be.

Sissy had indeed brought a cake. Something fancy with fruit and glaze on it.

"No way you made that yourself," Lily muttered. Sissy wasn't much in the kitchen. And she should have known it was much fancier than a teenager boy cared for it to be.

Jean's turkey looked tastier than usual. It was easy to match that dish with Jean's card. A half-dozen others, and Lily was left with only Audrey's card and one with absolutely awful handwriting that looked like it might even be the work of teenage girls.

Even the teenagers were flaunting their baked goods along with their bodies these days?

The two dishes left were a container of homemade macaroni salad and a baked chicken thing.

With that body, Audrey probably didn't touch carbs, Lily reasoned. The baked chicken was likely hers.

She decided to ask Jake just in case. After all, he wouldn't have forgotten Audrey in that little outfit. Whether it had blinded him to everything else, including what she brought, Lily didn't know, but she'd find out.

She took the container of baked chicken to show Jake, opened the kitchen door and there was Nick.

She had to work fast to keep the chicken from landing on the ground. He was more worried about her landing on the ground, because while she caught the pan of chicken, he caught her with lightning reflexes and the kind of strength she couldn't help but admire.

She'd have pitched backward, if not for him.

As it was, he had her, his big hands on her upper arms holding her easily, a wry, maybe slightly amused expression on her face.

"Lily," he said, much too close. "You okay?"

"Yes," she whispered.

"Sorry I startled you."

His hands lingered for a long moment, her arms feeling odd and tingly. Only once he was sure she was firmly planted on her feet, did he let her go and he step back.

"No. It was me. I wasn't looking where I was going," she admitted, a funny little catch in her voice, finding herself oddly breathless and seeing nothing but wide shoulders and well-muscles arms.

Feeling pure heat coming off his body.

Not such a shock, she decided.

After all, she hadn't been this close to a man other than her ex-husband in years. So she supposed it wasn't all that surprising.

She blinked up at him, a little confused and a lot embarrassed and…she wasn't even sure what else.

What had she been thinking? Doing? Saying? Her mind was a blank.

"I doubt you're the kind of woman to come over here and steal baked chicken, so…"

"Oh," she rushed in. "No. I wasn't. I swear."

"I didn't think you were, Lily."

No. He just probably thought she was nuts. "Jake got a little confused about which dish came from who, and I told him I'd help him sort it out."

"Yeah. He ripped off the cards and lids and was eating out of the pans before he even thought about keeping track of who brought what."

Lily nodded. "He seems like a really sweet kid. He's at my house, to make sure my girls don't wake up and find themselves alone. I'm sure I know who brought everything except this and one other thing."

She held up the baked chicken.

"I remember that one," he said.

"A woman wearing…"

"Next to nothing," he said plainly and if anything, a bit confused by it all.

"Shorts and a…"

"Bra-like thing," he said.

"Audrey Graham," Lily said, turning around and heading back into the kitchen. "I'll just put her card with this dish, and—"

"Does she often show up at strangers' doors dressed like that?" he asked.

Lily laughed, couldn't help it, then reminded herself that she might not have dressed as provocatively as Audrey and the rest of the neighborhood ladies, but she'd been first in line at his door this morning.

What did that say about her?

What did it make him think about her? That she was just like all the others?

"Well…Audrey is…I guess you could say…she's turned into a physical fitness buff since her divorce was final." It was the kindest thing Lily could come up with to say. "She runs most every day now, and it's been so hot, so…"

She turned around, having finished labeling dishes, and found Nick Malone leaning against the kitchen counter, looking like a man with a lot of questions he wasn't sure he wanted answered.

"Friendly neighborhood," he said.

"Yes. Very."

"I've never lived in a place like this. Didn't expect such a welcome," he said carefully, like they were treading all around all sorts of subjects now. "Is it always like this when someone moves in?"

"Well…" She supposed she should warn him. Or give him the good news, depending on how he felt about things. "There aren't a lot of single men in the neighborhood."

"Okay," he said, looking even more confused.

"Mostly married couples and divorced mothers," she explained.

Lonely, divorced mothers.

Mothers with certain unmet needs.

Of which, she wouldn't have said she was one. Would have said she was fine. In need of nothing. Wanting nothing except a long, hot bubble bath and a good book.

And now here she was, with a gorgeous neighbor and that funny, slight fever again that she'd proven to herself wasn't a fever. At least not the first two times she'd taken her temperature today.

Lily looked up at him as innocently as she could manage.

"And all those women who showed up today are single?" he asked, like the idea frightened him a bit.

"No. Not all of them," Lily said, and then thought that meant she'd spent all day watching his house from her kitchen window.

Wait…no. That she'd looked at all the cards that came with the food.

She hoped that's what he thought she meant.

Not that she was spying.

"They're just…always happy to welcome a new neighbor," she said.

New man, she'd meant, but hadn't said it. Though he had to know that's what she meant. He could have a different woman for every day of the week, if he wanted, if she was any judge of what just happened today.

Did he want that? A rotation of different women from Sunday to Saturday?

Was he that kind of guy?

And what about Jake? Surely he wouldn't have women parading through the house with Jake here?

"Well, Jake is certainly happy," he said finally. "Unfortunately, I'm not much of a cook and neither is he."

"So, this is a good thing. All this…friendliness and neighborliness."

Was that even a word? *Neighborliness?*

Like this was about nothing but food.

Lily was embarrassing herself and a little confused.

Did the man not know how good he looked? Especially with his shirt off? Surely this wasn't the only place where women flirted with him?

Was there a world out there somewhere, outside of Lily's existence in the suburbs, where this man wouldn't be admired for his physique?

She couldn't imagine that there was.

Granted, she'd lived a fairly sheltered existence of kids' birthday parties and neighborhood cookouts and volunteering at her kids' schools, but she wasn't that out of it. Was she?

Not that she was going to ask *him* about any of this.

He probably thought *she* was one of *them*.

Not as blatant as Audrey Graham and her little jog-bra, but still one of them.

And maybe Lily was.

"Well, I'd better get back," Lily said, slipping past him and out the door, trying not to look like she was fleeing.

"Thanks for everything," Nick said.

"You're welcome. I hope the two of you like it here." Not a woman-a-day kind of like it here, but…like it. She blushed just thinking about him and what he might do with all those women. "I'll send Jake right home."

Chapter Three

Four days later, Nick waited just inside the front door of his new house. It was just before sunrise, and he was dressed to go running, but instead he was peeking out the front window like a man expecting to be accosted in the early-morning light, right here in one of the quietest subdivisions in town.

Not by a mugger, but a grown woman in a jog-bra.

She'd followed him for the whole five miles he'd run two days ago, followed him through the quiet streets, talking the whole time, when he'd been counting on clearing out his head of everything, on having a time when he had to do nothing but keep breathing and putting one foot in front of the other. And if that wasn't enough, the woman had followed him home, followed him inside.

Before he'd known what she was up to, she'd been all over him, right there in the kitchen. Okay, he'd been pretty sure what she was up to. He just didn't expect to be attacked in his own kitchen that morning, and before he could do anything about it, Jake had walked in. Though starving and still half-asleep, the kid had nearly gotten an eyeful.

Something Nick did not care to repeat.

He also didn't want anybody chattering to him the whole time he ran.

Which was why he was staring out the window, wondering if Audrey Graham was out there, waiting for him, despite the fact that he'd told her—politely but plainly—that he wasn't interested.

Obviously, whatever he'd said, it hadn't been enough.

"What are you doing?" Jake asked from behind him.

Nick nearly jumped out of his skin.

Too many years in the army before he joined the FBI.

Jake yawned. "Sorry. I forgot."

"One day, you're going to sneak up on me, and I'm going to crush your throat before I figure out who you are," Nick told him.

"You can really do that?" Jake asked admiringly.

"In a heartbeat," Nick boasted, hoping the kid would believe him and remember the warning next time. He'd really come close to hurting him once already when Jake startled him.

"Sorry. I thought you heard me." Jake shrugged, like the possibility of a crushed throat was no big deal. "So, what are you doing? Did you go run?"

"Not yet."

All of a sudden, Jake looked very interested. "Wait a minute? You're not…you know. Sneaking somebody out of the house, are you?"

"Sneaking someone out?" Nick repeated.

"You know. Like…a woman?"

"No, I am not sneaking a woman out of the house," Nick said.

"'Cause, if you want somebody to sleep over, I'm fine with that. Is it that Audrey woman? The one with the giant—" Jake lifted his hands up and held them about a foot away from his chest. "And the really cute daughter? 'Cause, I'd really like to know the daughter."

"No, it's not her. It's not anybody."

"Not anybody I know, huh? Okay—" Jake looked way too interested.

"Not anyone at all. No one was here. I wouldn't do that."

Nick started to say not with Jake in the house, but that sounded a bit hypocritical. Was he supposed to pretend to be a monk? Just because he was single and raising a kid? One who happened to be a teenage boy, no doubt with raging hormones of his own?

Nick didn't think so, but what did he know about the etiquette of single parents and their sex lives?

Not much.

He'd never been seriously involved with a woman with kids.

Hardly been seriously involved with any woman.

"So, you're just going to do without until I'm eighteen?" Jake asked, like he couldn't quite believe it. "'Cause I thought you'd be really cool about things like that. I thought...you know. You'd bring your ladies over here, and I'd bring mine, and we'd both be cool with that."

Nick did a double take. "You have ladies? Plural?"

"Well, not exactly," Jake said. "Not at the moment."

"Okay, one? You have one? Who you intend to entertain in your bedroom? At fifteen?"

"Well...maybe."

"No way that's gonna happen," Nick insisted.

"Really?" He looked crushed.

"Really," Nick said, barking out the word.

"Jeez," Jake grumbled, looking all put out. "I thought—"

"Well, you thought wrong."

Jake grumbled as he made his way into the kitchen, no doubt hungry already. After all, it had been a whole six hours or so since he'd eaten. Nick had found him in the kitchen at midnight, gulping down a giant bowl of cereal. Now the kid was already up and hungry again.

Nick couldn't sneak a woman into and out of this house, even if he'd wanted to. Jake got hungry too often to make that work.

And had ideas of entertaining, all of his own.

"Jesus!" Nick said, more of a prayer for help and understanding than anything else. "What am I supposed to do about that?"

And he couldn't even go for a decent run, because when he opened up the door to do that, he saw Audrey lurking behind a tree at the house next door, looking for him, no doubt.

Nick slammed the door and wondered if he could wait her out.

Didn't the woman have to go to work? Or take care of her kids? Did she have nothing better to do than stalk him?

He'd either have to find a way to avoid her, by finding out her schedule and running at a different time, or convince her he wasn't interested, and he'd bet she hadn't heard that from many red-blooded American males. It might be hard to convince her it was true.

"Damn," he muttered.

He was mowing the grass later that morning when Lily pulled into her driveway and got out of her little SUV, neither of her kids in sight.

He waved and kept on mowing, wanting the job done before it got too hot. But then he saw her open the back of her SUV and start wresting with a pile of wooden trim, and he cut off the mower and went to help.

"Here," he said, coming up behind her and catching an errant piece that was dragging on the ground. "Let me help."

"Oh." She whirled around, but the trim wasn't all the way out of the vehicle and didn't quite move with her.

Nick had to move fast to keep it from going all over the place and from hitting the ground and getting scuffed up.

"Sorry. Didn't mean to startle you," he said, wondering if she was naturally jumpy or a bit of a klutz.

"No. You didn't. I just…forgot I was holding all that and then…well, you know the rest."

"I've got it. Let me carry it in for you," he said, wiping the sweat off his face with his forearm and hoping the trim didn't slide out of his hands.

"Okay. Thanks."

She fished out her keys and headed for the back door, leading him through the kitchen and into the dining room, the top half of the walls freshly painted a muted gold tone and ready for the wide, white trim.

"Anywhere here is fine," she told him.

He piled the wood in the far corner. "You doing all this work yourself?"

"Yes. I like it. I used to be an interior decorator, but I found out I liked making all the decorating decisions myself, much better than following someone else's orders, and I like doing the physical work on a house myself. So after the girls were born, I started rehabbing houses and selling them."

He looked around at the room in progress and the kitchen that she'd obviously already done. "You do good work, Lily," he said.

"Thanks. How are you? How's Jake?"

"Jake's…as good as can be expected, I think," he said. "But what do I know? How do you think he is?"

"Sweet. Smart. Eager to please," she said. "He offered to mow my lawn in exchange for another batch of fudge."

"Hey, sorry—"

"No, it's great. I get tired of mowing the lawn, especially by this time of year. Believe me, it's worth a lot more to me than a plate of fudge to have someone else do it."

"You're sure?"

"Absolutely." She walked into the kitchen and grabbed a couple of glasses from the cabinet. "Would you like something to drink? You look like you've been out there in the heat for a while."

"Water. Thank you."

She handed him a glass, which he downed in one, long swallow. She watched as he did it, looking like she wasn't quite sure what to make of him or if he made her uneasy or something.

But then she just smiled and refilled his glass again.

"So, if it's all right with you, I'll make a deal with Jake? Food in exchange for lawn-mowing duty?"

"Fine with me. Just don't let him take advantage of you or your time."

She shrugged, smiled a bit nervously. "I like to cook, and it's just as easy to make something for five people as it is for me and the girls. What's his favorite meal?"

"I don't even know," Nick said. One more thing he didn't know about kids in general and this one in particular. "I mean, I haven't found anything the kid won't eat. I do remember being at my sister's a year or so ago, and she'd made a pot roast. Jake ate plates full. I came into the kitchen not an hour and a half later to get something to drink and found the pan of leftovers still on the stove, cooling I guess, and Jake was eating out of the pan. Kid's got no manners when it comes to food, and that he could be hungry again after eating so much at dinner…"

Nick just shook his head in wonder.

"Okay," Lily said. "A pot roast, it is. Everything else going okay?"

Nick hesitated, needing to talk to someone, but…Lily?

He didn't know her that well, and as open about their sexuality as some women were these days, he suspected Lily wasn't one of them. She seemed sweet and a little shy, and Jake had volunteered that she hadn't been divorced from her husband for that long.

Nick just couldn't see asking her how she handled her sex life with two little girls in the house.

"I'd like to help, if I could," she said, all sweetness and earnestness.

Nick frowned, thinking he could at least find out a little more about Audrey Graham to help him avoid her.

"Well…" He hesitated. "I don't think there's any easy way to say this, and I really don't want to make you uncomfortable, but…"

Ahhh!
Lily thought she was going to die of embarrassment right there on the spot.
He knew!
He knew she'd been practically slobbering all over him, and he wanted to talk about it?

"Ahhh," she whimpered.

She didn't mean to. Not out loud at least, but she must have, because suddenly, he looked concerned. He took her by the arm and said, "Lily? You okay?"

"Yes," she lied and not at all convincingly.

"You sure?" he asked.

"Yes. Really. Just go ahead. Tell me. It's about—"

"Audrey Graham," he said, looking like it pained him to even say the name to her.

"Oh! Audrey?" Lily smiled, so relieved she could have fallen to her knees and said a prayer of gratitude right then.

She'd been certain he knew she'd been all but drooling over him while he moved in and then while he'd been doing yard work the other day. She was so grateful it hadn't gotten that hot yet, and he still had his shirt on this morning.

Him shirtless in her kitchen was probably more than she could have handled.

"Yes, Audrey. Did you say something about her running every morning?"

"Yes," she said.

Did he want to watch?

Because the woman was certainly putting on a show.

Her outfits got skimpier by the day. She must have gone shopping after Nick moved in.

Someone had even said Nick and Audrey had run together the day before, and that when it was over, Audrey had followed Nick into his house. But people said a lot of things, and Lily made a policy to discount at least half of what she heard, just on principle alone, and it must have been one of the few occasions when Lily hadn't been watching his house, because she hadn't seen a thing.

"Do you know where she runs? Like how far and the route she takes?" Nick asked, looking really uncomfortable with the question.

"Not really. I'm not a runner. I mean, I see her go by our houses sometimes," Lily said.

More often, now that Nick moved in.

Did that mean he hadn't run with her the other day?

"And…uh…I guess there's no easy way to say this, but…if I wanted to run without…running into her?"

"Oh," Lily said, relieved, but puzzled.

He wanted to avoid a woman with a body like Audrey's?

She didn't think anybody who looked like him would want to avoid someone who looked like Audrey.

"I like to run alone," he said. "That's all. Really. It's just time to clear my head, and she followed me the other day and…well, she talked the whole time."

"Oh. Of course." Lily nodded, gleeful at the thought of Audrey, half-dressed and nearly bouncing out of her bra and annoying Nick every step of the way.

It shouldn't make Lily so happy, because Audrey's husband had walked out on her just like Lily's had, and Lily knew how awful that was. Lily felt bad for everything Audrey had gone through, but still… She didn't want Audrey to have Nick.

"If you cut through my backyard on the side farthest from yours, then take the first left, then a right, it will take you out of the neighborhood the back way. From there, you might be able to run without seeing her, because I think she stays in the subdivision."

He grinned. "That would be great. Thanks."

"Sure," she said. "Anytime."

He looked like there might be more he wanted to say, but then thought better of it and just put his empty glass down on the counter and said, "Well, I guess I'd better be going, finish the lawn before it gets any hotter."

"Okay."

Lily went to open the door for him, and he reached for it at the same time, which meant they ended up almost bumping into each other, and when they pulled away, she went left and he went right.

Which meant, they ended up even closer.

He gave a little chuckle. "Hang on." And caught her by the arms, to keep her from moving again the same way he did, she thought.

Which was fine.

It was…almost a polite gesture.

Nothing more.

She didn't move at first, didn't want to if she was honest with herself, just stood there breathing in the scent of him, a big, strong man who'd been outside doing manly things, and the sheer heat of him, which seemed to be radiating from his body.

And then he froze. "Damn," he muttered, turning his head back to her.

"What's wrong?"

Had she done something? Completely given herself away?

Would she be forever embarrassed in his company and have to live with him being right next door forever and knowing she wanted him as much as Audrey? Would he be getting tips from someone else on how to avoid Lily?

Still, he held her gently by the arms, mere fractions of an inch from being pressed up against him, and he wasn't moving away.

"Audrey's out there. I saw her through the kitchen door," he said.

"Oh."

"And she sees us," he said.

Okay?

So?

"I don't understand—"

"Lily, she followed me into the kitchen two mornings ago and practically jumped me as Jake was coming downstairs."

"Oh!"

"I thought I made it clear, as politely as possible, that I wasn't interested, but maybe I didn't. Because she's been stalking me ever since, and Jake is daydreaming about going out with her daughter. So I'd rather not piss her off completely, if I don't have to."

"Okay." Lily said, still frozen there, half an inch from him and liking it. Liking it a lot. "But what does that have to do with…this?"

He took a breath, chest and shoulders rising, coming that much closer to actually touching her, and she wanted him to touch her. She was tingling all over, like her body was singing, it was so happy. Like she'd already anticipated this slight touch a dozen times in the few seconds they'd been standing here, her waiting and waiting for things she couldn't bring herself to ask for.

He was just so big and strong. So much…a man.

And it had been so long since she'd been this close to a man.

If she was really honest with herself, she'd admit she'd never been this close to a man as appealing as him. In a completely physical way, of course. She didn't really know him. She just knew that her body really wanted to know his better.

"Well," he said, dipping his head ever so slowly until his lips were resting somewhere near the base of her throat.

Not touching her.

Not really.

Doing something oh so sexy that was almost like touching.

Breathing on her, breathing in her, like a man taking a moment to savor a great meal he knew he was going to love before he ever took the first bite.

Bite!

She couldn't think about him taking a *bite* of her.

Men didn't take bites of her!

She wasn't that kind of girl.

Maybe she should have been.

Maybe she regretted that right this minute, but still…

"If I could just do this for a moment," he whispered, his arms sliding carefully around her.

"Mmm-hmm," she said, her voice coming out a little squeaky and weird.

"And you were to put your arms around me, just for a minute…."

"Okay." She was all too happy to comply.

She'd been thinking about touching him for days. Touching him in all sorts of ways, in all sorts of places that made her blush.

And actually touching him was even better, she found.

His body was solid as could be, all hard and sexy, muscles curving and sloping one into another, her hands sliding up his biceps, to cup his broad shoulders, one hand even sneaking onto the base of his neck and into the ends of his hair.

"There you go," he said, like he really liked that. "Just like that."

Oh, yes.

Just like that.

Lily took a giant gulp of air, her breasts rising to the point where they just barely brushed his chest.

He sucked in a breath, then gave a shaky little laugh.

"She's watching everything we do," he said. "And if it's okay with you, I think if I just do this for a few moments…."

And then he stroked the tip of his nose along the side of her neck, lips so close they left a trail of heat and longing in their wake.

Lily whimpered. Couldn't help it.

If this didn't stop soon, she'd be begging him to stop putting on a show for Audrey and just kiss her already and be done with it.

As it was, she could imagine his mouth opening and then landing right there in that spot where the base of her neck met her shoulder, a spot that was already tingling with longing. She thought about his warm, moist mouth teasing, caressing, his beautiful, hard body plastered up against hers.

Lily stretched her neck out to the side, like she was giving him that spot, giving him anything he wanted, and let her body settle in against his. His arms tightened around her ever so slowly and carefully, like he was determined not to take advantage of the situation.

Or she hoped that's what it was.

That he was a nice man.

A very nice, wickedly sexy man.

His nose nuzzled her ear, teased her hair, his hand cupping one side of her face and his lips settling as gently as a whisper against her temple before he slowly drew back, a wry grin on his face.

Lily tried not to whimper or to beg for more. Tried to stand on her own two feet without any help from him and tried not to look too thrilled by what he'd done or too devastated that it was over.

"So…she got an eyeful?" Lily asked, reminding herself what this had all been about.

"Yes, she did." He grinned easily, the way a man might look at a woman he considers a good friend. "I hope that was okay? I mean, I hope I didn't offend you…."

"No. Of course not," she said. "Anything to help out a neighbor."

"Well, she's gone so…" He waited, like he wanted to say more.

She waited, too, hoping, wanting, needing, thrilled and a little bit scared.

But then he shook his head and all he said was, "I should be getting back to work. Thanks again, Lily."

"You're welcome," she said.

She waited until he was out the door and she heard his lawn mower start before she sank down to the floor in her kitchen, leaning back against the cabinets, closed her eyes and relived every glorious second of what had just happened.

Sadly, it was the sexiest thing that had happened to her in years.

Chapter Four

Jake hadn't been trying to spy on them.

Honestly.

He'd been spying on Audrey Graham, the woman who wore all the skimpy tops and had practically attacked his uncle in their kitchen, because Mrs. Graham had an absolutely gorgeous sixteen-year-old daughter, clearly miles out of Jake's league and who'd never so much as looked down her nose at him at school.

But still…a guy had to have hope, didn't he?

If nothing else, Jake could look and hope.

At the moment, he'd been looking at Mrs. Graham, hoping her daughter might be with her, but she wasn't. He'd seen Mrs. Graham staring into Lily's house and looking none too happy at what she saw, and then Jake wondered what was going on, and that's when he saw them.

His uncle and Lily?

It looked like Nick was licking Lily's neck or something, and it sure looked like Lily liked it.

Women liked to have their necks licked?

Jake frowned.

He didn't exactly know a ton about women, but he'd sure never heard that one.

Kissing necks, yes.

Licking?

Not that he had a problem trying it.

He was open to pretty much anything, especially with Andie Graham.

He would be her willing slave, fulfilling her every wish, if he ever got to the point where she knew he was alive and was willing to have him close enough to do things to that pretty neck of hers.

Jake took one more look at his uncle and Lily, not quite sure what he thought about that. One, he didn't want his uncle to make Andie's mother mad, just on the off chance that Andie might one day have anything to do with Jake. And he liked Lily. She was sweet, and she'd been kind and understanding and made the most incredible fudge Jake had ever eaten. He didn't want anyone to hurt her, and if she knew his uncle was all over Mrs. Graham in the kitchen the other day, and now all over Lily, Lily wouldn't like that. Would she?

Women didn't like to share.

It was one thing Jake was pretty sure about.

And he didn't like thinking his uncle was the kind of man who'd hurt someone like Lily. Was he that kind of man? Jake frowned and—

"Excuse me? I'm looking for the Malone house? Is this it?"

Jake thought for a second he must be dreaming, because he was pretty sure he knew that voice. He *dreamed* about that voice. About more than the voice.

He turned around really slowly and hoped he didn't look too stupid as he stared for a minute and wondered if he was actually dreaming or if Andie Graham was actually standing in front of him. If she'd actually spoken to him.

"Uh…" was all he managed to get out before he had to take a breath and try to calm down.

She was wearing some really short shorts and a little white top with spaghetti straps and a scooped out neckline, and truly, it was hard to breathe this close to her. Especially with her looking the way she did. Looking as good as she did.

Had to be a fantasy come true.

She was looking for *his* house?

"No way," he muttered, out loud he feared.

She gave him an odd look, one he no doubt deserved, like he might have the IQ of a piece of fruit.

"The Malone house?" he repeated, his voice doing that weird, cracking thing that it hadn't done since he was fourteen. He hated that stupid cracking thing.

She nodded, like she feared words might be too much for him.

"That's my house," he said, still thinking this had to be a mistake.

No way she'd come looking for him.

She frowned, like maybe she didn't believe him or was really confused. "Your dad is Nick Malone?"

"Uncle," he said, his voice still sounding funny.

"Oh. And this is your house?" She pointed to Lily's.

"No, this one," he said, nodding in the other direction.

"Oh. Okay. I was actually…" She looked thoroughly exasperated, not so much like the blond princess of his fantasies. More like a real person who might actually have normal problems like everyone else. "I was looking for my mom."

And she didn't like admitting that. Or maybe it was…thinking her mom was here with his uncle? That something was going on between them?

"She's right over…" It was Jake's turn to frown. She wasn't there anymore. "She was there just a minute ago."

Andie sighed, like she dreaded the next part, then asked, "Do you think she went inside?"

"No. My uncle's not there," Jake told her, not adding that his uncle was at Lily's, licking Lily's neck or something like that, and that Andie's mom had seen them and hadn't been happy about it.

"Oh," Andie said, sighing once again. "Your uncle? Is he married?"

"No," Jake said. Why would she care if his uncle was married?

"Well...thanks, I guess. I'll just... I'll be..." She paused for one more moment, then looked him over one more time. "Do I know you?"

Jake shook his head, then woke up to the fact that this was his chance. She knew he was alive, even if it was just to help her find his house. "I'm Jake. Jake Elliott. We go to the same school. I mean...I'm pretty sure we do. Jefferson?"

"Yeah, I go to Jefferson. What are you? What year?"

"Sophomore," he admitted, knowing she was a junior.

Just one more way in which she was way out of his league.

"Oh," she said. "Well, I've got to go find my mom. See you."

Jake mumbled goodbye, and then was treated to the sight of her walking away from him in those short shorts, with those long, tanned legs, her long, blond hair swinging as she walked, wishing he could start this whole conversation over again and not sound like an idiot, not act like one, not be one.

She'd talked to him.

She knew his name and where he lived.

Jake suspected he'd be dreaming of her tonight, dreaming in more vivid detail than ever before.

Okay, maybe that wasn't the best idea I've ever had, Nick told himself, safely back in his own house, out of sight of any prying eyes and not mere centimeters away from being plastered up against Lily.

Luscious Lily.

He made a face, trying to get that particular description out of his head.

He did not need to be thinking of his neighbor as *luscious.*

Particularly with a teenage boy in the house who had visions of entertaining his own ladies in his bedroom.

So, no…nuzzling Lily's neck was definitely not a good idea. It had just felt like one.

A great one.

Nick tried to breathe and turn his thoughts to something else, anything else but how long it had been since he'd been involved with a woman or had one in his bed and the utter unlikelihood that he'd ever talk Lily Tanner into joining him there.

Audrey, of the skimpier and skimpier jogging outfits, he could have, if he wanted her. Which, unfortunately, he didn't.

Lily, he suspected, was firmly off-limits.

He'd bet the woman had never had casual sex in her life. She was too sweet, too nice, too kindhearted. Softhearted, he was sure.

Not at all his type.

And yet…pretty was the word that came to mind, and it both seemed to fit and not do her justice at the same time. She had pretty blond hair and gorgeous skin, an easy smile and an openness and genuineness. She seemed real. That's what it was. Not fussy. Not fake. Not pushy. Not playing any kind of games. Real and nice and surprisingly appealing.

He opened up the refrigerator and poured a cold glass of water from the pitcher he kept there, wishing it was that easy to cool himself down.

Damn, Lily.

She'd felt so soft and fragile beneath his hands, smelled so good, trembled ever so slightly, blushed a bit, and all he'd been able to think about was devouring her right there in her kitchen.

He took a long swallow of that cold water, but it didn't seem to do anything to cool him down.

One by one, he thought of all the women who'd shown up at his door with offerings of food, drink and, though unspoken, companionship. Surely he could think of one he'd like to kill some time with, one who wouldn't object at all to killing time with him.

And yet he found himself discarding one after another and staring out the window toward Lily's house.

He'd just have to stay away from her. That was all there was to it.

He had Jake to take care of, parenting stuff to figure out, legal issues to sort through having to do with his sister and brother-in-law's estate, determining the boys' finances and whether there was enough money to see them all through college and if there was time, his own life to see to.

More than enough to do to keep a grown man busy and his mind off one, quietly pretty, sweet-smelling woman.

Yeah. He'd just have to stay away from her.

Three days later, Lily was trying to explain to Jake the finer points of scraping old wallpaper off the kitchen wall, when he started asking her about Audrey Graham.

What did she know about Mrs. Graham?

Lily frowned.

Was the woman still chasing after Nick? Even after the... *incident?*

Lily was trying very hard not to call it what it was.

Neck-nuzzling.

Oh! She practically shivered, just thinking about it. How good it had been. How delicious it had felt.

Better than sweet, warm, gooey fudge, as far as Lily was concerned.

"You do know her, don't you?" Jake said again, giving her a funny look.

Like she'd gone off into la-la land.

"Yes," Lily all but groaned. "I know her. Is she...bothering uncle?"

hated asking the question, but there it was. It had just

popped out, oh so innocently. Okay, not so innocent. Probably not innocently at all. She felt really bad about it, but there! She'd asked.

Jake looked puzzled. "I don't know. Maybe."

Lily went back to steaming the wallpaper in hopes it would just peel off the wall, wishing quite firmly that she hadn't asked. She hadn't seen Audrey Graham lurking around the Malone house, but that didn't mean it hadn't happened. Audrey was sneaky and quite determined. There was no telling what Lily had missed.

And then she wondered if maybe Jake was trying to look out for her, to warn her that Audrey had been hanging around, and maybe she wasn't bothering Nick. Maybe Nick was enjoying himself.

Maybe he'd changed his mind after the neck-nuzzling incident. Maybe Audrey had done something to change his mind.

Lily made a face, then tried to wipe the look off her face before Jake saw.

She really hated the idea of Nick with Audrey Graham. Having to see them next door. Hear them. Think about them.

Nick neck-nuzzling with Audrey Graham.

Lily wasn't sure if she wanted to scream or cry.

"Are you okay?" Jake asked.

"Of course," Lily lied, not too badly she hoped.

"So…Mrs. Graham has a daughter, right?" Jake asked, as he scraped the wall clean of the residue left on it, despite Lily's careful steaming and peeling off of the old wallpaper.

Daughter?

"Yes," Lily said. Had she completely misread the whole conversation so far? Was she so obsessed with Nick Malone that she'd completely jumped to the wrong conclusions? "I think she probably goes to high school with you."

Jake turned an interesting shade of pink, and Lily didn't think it was coming from the heat of the steamer.

Okay, now she got it.

The Graham women captivated men of all ages.

Lily rolled her eyes. "Andie," she said. "You know Andie?"

"Well…yeah. I mean, I doubt she remembers I'm alive. But…I've seen her around."

Oh, I just bet you have, Lily thought.

She tried to think of the last time she'd seen Andie Graham and if the daughter took after the mother in her wardrobe choices.

Lily hoped not, for Jake's sake.

"Isn't she a little old for you, Jake?" Lily tried, because he was so adorably awkward and sweet, and if Andie was anything like her mother, she'd chew him up and spit him out without thinking twice about it. Lily hated to see him hurt.

"Only a year older," Jake said.

Lily nodded.

"Do you know…like…what she likes to do? I mean, where she might hang out? Or anything like that?" Jake asked.

"I think I've seen her at the mall a few times," Lily told him.

Andie really looked like a mall kind of girl.

She had a feeling Jake would be spending every spare moment there, hoping to run into Andie.

Trying to let him down easily, Lily told him, "I think, last I heard, she had a boyfriend who's in college now. Someone who went to her high school last year."

"Oh." Jake looked completely dejected.

A college boy.

Lily kept steaming. Jake attacked the wall, scraping so hard Lily was afraid he was going to gouge the Sheetrock underneath.

"Hey, why don't we take a break while I start dinner, okay?" she suggested.

"Dinner?" He perked right up at that.

"What would you like?" Lily asked, shutting off her steamer and heading for the refrigerator. "Come on. You can pick."

If he couldn't have Andie Graham, he could at least have a good dinner.

They dug through Lily's refrigerator, Jake settling on a chicken and rice dish Lily had made last week that he'd particularly enjoyed. She'd bought twice as much as she had the week before, astonished at how much he could eat and wanting to have enough to send home to Nick, too, and maybe for leftovers.

She'd learned Nick and Jake lived on takeout and her leftovers, and decided she was going to teach Jake to cook. Otherwise, they might not survive.

He was cutting up chicken, and Lily was assembling ingredients when the girls burst into the kitchen, arguing as they went.

"Cannot!" Ginny said, heading for the refrigerator.

"Can, too!" Brittany said, her bottom lip sticking out in a pout so adorable, it was all Lily could do not to laugh.

It was a good thing she looked cute when she pouted, because she pouted a lot and whined. The whining got really old, but the cute pout often saved Lily from getting too irritated.

"Cannot!" Ginny said, standing in the open refrigerator and blocking her sister's view of all the goodies inside.

"Can, too!" Brittany folded her arms and glared at her sister.

"What is it that Brittany cannot do?" Lily asked, giving her oldest daughter a look that used to have the power to silence her instantly, but was quickly losing that magical effect.

"She cannot have a horse for her birthday! She doesn't get a present like that!" Ginny said.

A horse?

Lily gaped at her baby girl, tears filling her eyes now as she tried to turn on the charm and get her way.

"Oh, honey," Lily said. "A horse?"

Brittany nodded hopefully. "Mattie Wright got a horse, and a special outfit to wear to ride it and riding lessons for her birthday!"

"Mattie Wright's father owns half the county," Lily said. "Including a farm on the edge of town where Mattie's horse can live. We don't have a place where a horse could live. We just have the backyard."

"He could live there," Brittany said.

"Honey, it's just not big enough for a horse."

"We could get a little horse," Brittany reasoned. "A baby horse. He wouldn't need much room."

Ginny started laughing at that. "A baby horse? You are so silly. A baby horse grows up into a big horse, Britt. Everybody knows that."

Brittany glared at her and started to cry.

Jake jumped in then, trying to help. "You know, Brittany, horses are really big. They can be kind of scary. One of my brothers was on a horse once, and he fell off and the horse stepped on him and broke his nose."

Brittany looked highly skeptical. "Did he really?"

Jake nodded. "Maybe it would be better to wait until you're bigger to have a horse."

Jake looked to Lily to see if that was a mistake or not. To imply she might get a horse later.

Lily nodded. Anything that got her daughter off the horse thing for now was okay with her.

"Isn't there anything else you'd like for your birthday?" Jake tried.

"Well." Brittany sighed, like it was quite a lot to ask, that she give up on the horse and go to her second choice. But she liked Jake and gave him an answer. "I thought about...a tree house."

Her eyes lit up once again, a new dream replacing the horse just that quickly.

Lily frowned once again. "A tree house?"

"Yeah," Brittany said, like it sounded like the greatest thing in the world.

"Oh. Great."

* * *

"Do you know anything about building tree houses?" Jake asked three nights later as they wolfed down take-out Chinese food for dinner.

Nick made a face. "You want a tree house?"

"No!" Jake looked disgusted. "Lily's daughter, the littlest one, Brittany, does. It's her birthday next week. I heard her talking to Lily about it when I was over there helping her with the wallpaper."

"Oh."

Lily.

Stay away from Lily.

Nick might need a flashing neon sign.

"So, do you know anything about 'em?" Jake asked.

"Not really. I mean, we had one when your mother and I were growing up, but it wasn't much more than a platform in a tree and a ladder to reach it."

"You think I could build one?" Jake said between shoveling a huge mouthful of curry chicken into his mouth.

"Have you ever built anything?"

"Not really."

"Then I don't think you should start with something in a tree. That's something you want to get right, especially if little girls are going to climb up there and play in it."

"That's what Lily said," Jake mumbled, mouth still half-full. "That she wasn't sure if she trusted herself to do it and have it be safe for Brittany. I mean, Lily knows how to do lots of stuff. She's fixing up her house all by herself and everything, but I guess the tree thing is different."

"Yeah," Nick said, thinking, *Stay away, stay away, stay away.*

If he could quit thinking about her neck, that would be even better.

"So, could you do it?"

"I don't know if that's a good idea, Jake," Nick said, trying to think of what he could use as an excuse, other than the fact that he'd decided Lily was hot and that he was getting really lonely fast.

"Why not?" The kid dumped the last of what Nick had thought was an impressive pile of chicken and rice onto his plate and resumed eating at a rapid pace.

Nick frowned.

"Did you want some of this?" Jake asked, holding out his plate.

"No. I'm good. Go ahead."

Gotta order more food next time, Nick told himself.

More food.

And stay away from Lily.

He could do those things.

"So…I don't get it. Why is it a bad idea?" Jake asked.

"I just…have a lot to do," Nick said. "We're barely settled in here, and I have things to take care of."

Best Nick could come up with.

He wondered if the kid could see straight through him and knew Nick was just trying to avoid Lily and why, but Jake just gave him an odd look.

"It's just that the poor kid's had a tough year, you know?" Jake said. "Her father moving out on them. And it's her birthday. She wanted a horse, but Lily said that was impossible, and the next thing she wanted was a tree house, and… I don't know. I just don't want her to be sad on her birthday. She's a little bitty kid, and she lost her dad, and… I just wanted to try to help."

Jake was practically in tears by the end of it, and Nick had a feeling they were talking about more than Lily's daughter feeling bad because her father moved out.

He had a feeling they were talking at least in part about Jake losing both a mother and a father and feeling pretty lousy about it and wishing there was something that would make him feel better.

If Nick knew what it was, he'd give it to the kid in a heartbeat.

A horse, a tree house…not on Jake's list, Nick was sure.

But it was sweet that the kid was thinking of Lily's little girl and what she'd lost and wanting to try to make it better.

He was a good kid.

A really good kid with a good heart.

Nick looked at him for a long time. Should he pat the kid on the back? Or do one of those manly, nonhug kind of things that men did, like hit him on the shoulder or something. Or did this call for an all-out hug?

Nick wasn't sure.

He wasn't sure about anything, so he just said the first thing he thought of.

"That's nice of you, Jake. To want to help her like that. Your mother would be proud of you."

Jake's head came up at that. "You think?"

"I know she would."

"So you'll help me help Lily with the tree house?" Jake asked, cornering him but good.

"We'll work something out," Nick said.

Maybe he could help without actually being there.

Help from a distance of some kind.

Or maybe Lily could leave, and he and Jake could build the thing, with Lily and her neck nowhere near them as they did it.

That was it.

Or something like that.

He just had to be strong.

Don't start anything.

And stay away from Luscious Lily.

Chapter Five

"So, big weekend alone, huh?" Marcy said suggestively over the phone to Lily, who was repacking for her girls' stay with their father. "What are you going to do?"

"Nothing, really," Lily said, wondering how her youngest expected to make it through the weekend with no socks, no underwear, no pajamas and three hair bows and a half a dozen toys. *Honestly.*

Lily dug into the sock and underwear drawer, grabbing a handful of both for Brittany.

"Lily, you can't just sit there and wait for life to come to you. You have to get out and meet it sometimes," Marcy claimed.

"I may meet my hairstylist and get my hair done," she said. Best she could do.

Marcy sighed heavily, as if Lily's life was such a chore that Marcy had to manage.

"I like getting my hair done!" Lily said.

Truly, she did.

It was nice and quiet in the salon, and she loved having someone else fuss over her hair. Just getting it washed felt good, and that little bit of scalp massage, and then having someone run their fingers through her hair….

It was Lily's turn to sigh in anticipation.

"There. What was that?" Marcy asked.

"That was me, thinking about getting my hair done. I really do like it."

"Is your hairdresser by any chance straight and male?"

Lily laughed, getting down on her hands and knees to look under the bed for Brittany's other shoe. "I wish!"

Having a cute, straight, single man fussing with her hair sounded really, really good.

She closed her eyes, seeing herself in the chair at the salon, practically purring with happiness, saw *him* smiling appreciatively at her in the salon mirror, felt big, strong, capable hands running through her hair….

Lily sighed once again, maybe groaned a bit.

Her imaginary hair-guy leaned down, lifting a handful of her hair to his face to smell it, then let his warm mouth settle against her neck. She watched in the mirror and then realized…

It was Nick.

"Ahhh!" Lily cried, coming out of her little stupor in the blink of an eye.

"Oh, wow. You must have a cute, straight hairdresser!" Marcy cried.

"I do not!" Lily insisted.

She had a cute—and she felt certain—straight neighbor who'd nearly nibbled on her neck to keep another woman away from him, and she'd been having wicked, wildly distracting thoughts about him ever since.

That was all.

"If you don't tell me everything right this minute—"

"Gotta go," Lily interrupted. "I hear Richard's car in the driveway."

"Spit on him for me," Marcy said. "Bye."

Lily got off the phone, grabbed the girls' bags and hurried downstairs, hating this whole exchange-of-the-children ritual. She tried to be civil, tried not to be nervous or mad or sad or anything, tried to be as neutral in her emotions and her speech as could be, and yet it was just so awkward and so hard.

To think that she and Richard would ever be shuffling their girls back and forth this way, disrupting their lives, changing everything, was still unbelievable.

The girls were in the family room playing on the computer. Lily yelled to them that their father had arrived as she carried their bags downstairs to the front door. She wanted to hand them over quickly, smiling somehow as she did it, and then hide in her house for a while, trying not to think of how quiet it was, how odd, how sad.

She made it outside, bags in hand, to find Richard standing on the driveway surveying the place like he was trying to figure out what it was worth at the moment, then looking uneasy as he saw her.

He pulled out his phone, checked it or at least pretended to, probably just trying to avoid talking to her, and then got a funny look on his face. Lily tried to remember what the admittedly handsome face had looked like when he'd so coldly told her he was walking out on her and the girls and had the nerve to think she shouldn't have been surprised or particularly upset. To remember that pretty packages didn't necessarily hold good things or good men inside of them, and that she didn't ever want to be fooled in that way again. That attraction could fizzle out and disappear so quickly, and a woman might be surprised at how little was left.

And then before she got too mad, she tried to just get the exchange over with.

"The girls are on their way," Lily said, talking too fast. "I double-checked their bags. They should have everything they need, including some cold medicine, in case Ginny's nose is stuffed up tonight. Don't worry. It's the grape-flavored kind. She likes it and won't give you a hard time about taking it. Dosage information is on the bottle. She weighs forty-six pounds—"

"Lily, wait—"

"Brittany's pillow, the one she won't sleep without, is in the bag. Please make sure it comes back with her on Sunday—"

"Lily, I'm trying to tell you—"

"And try not to load them up on sugar when you do the birthday thing with Brittany. A piece of cake at a restaurant is plenty—"

"Lily, I can't take them this weekend," he said.

She stopped talking at that, mouth hanging open, annoyance building inside of her like mercury rising in a thermometer on a scorching hot day. "What do you mean, you can't take them?"

"I mean, I can't. Something came up."

"Richard, it's Brittany's birthday!"

"Not until next Thursday. I'll come by then. Or the day before."

"You said you were going to take her to the zoo this weekend for her birthday. She's been looking forward to it for two weeks."

He didn't even have the grace to look embarrassed. "I'm sorry. I have a job to do."

"And you have a daughter who's turning seven!" she said, glaring at him.

Jake was home, standing in the kitchen with the door wide-open, staring outside, when Nick came downstairs to see if there were any leftovers from the previous night's dinner that had survived this long.

"Hey," Nick asked, grabbing a glass and hoping there was something to drink, too. "What's going on?"

Everything simply disappeared around Jake the human disposal unit.

"Lily's ex is giving her a hard time," Jake said, still standing there.

Nick turned around and went to stand behind the boy, staring at Lily on her driveway with a guy in a really expensive suit who was up in her face about something.

They weren't yelling, so Nick couldn't hear what was going on, but he didn't like how close the guy was or the look on his face.

"You sure it's the ex?" Nick asked.

"Yeah. He was supposed to take the girls this weekend, but he's backing out," Jake said, then looked like Nick might have thought he was doing something wrong. "I was walking home when he showed up, and I just wanted to make sure Lily was okay."

"Good for you," Nick told him, putting a hand on the kid's shoulder. "A man should always look out for a woman. Some of them won't ever thank you for it, because they think they're invincible, but they're not. And some men are just asses. This guy looks like one of 'em. What else did you hear?"

"He doesn't even want to go in and tell the girls himself that he's backing out on their weekend. He wants Lily to do it for him," Jake said.

Which meant Nick had a choice.

Stay away from Luscious Lily.

Stop wondering why that fool of a man would ever have left her, and stop being mad that he'd apparently decided to walk out on their kids this way, too.

Or go do something about it.

Nick definitely tended to be the kind of man who'd do something about it when anyone was doing something he didn't like to a woman.

And surely teaching her ex some manners was one thing he

could do without getting distracted by how much he wanted to nuzzle Lily's delectable neck.

Surely there was no danger here.

Still, he knew it was better to keep his distance, and Lily struck him as an immensely capable woman. She might not thank him for interfering. She might not even want him to know she was fighting with her ex about something like this.

"Let's give it a minute. See how this plays out," Nick said.

"Why? The guy's a real jerk," Jake said, still staring.

Now he had a scrawny, little finger that he was shaking in Lily's face, and then it looked like he was poking her in the shoulder with it, trying to get her to back away from him.

Nick saw red.

"You're right. We're not going to stand here and let him get away with that," Nick said. "Come on. Go to Lily's house. Get her girls and ask them to come outside."

Jake hesitated. "You're sure."

"Oh, yeah. This jerk can explain things to them himself, if he has the nerve," Nick said.

"But—"

"Go on. I'm right behind you. I'll handle him."

With pleasure, Nick decided.

With great pleasure.

Lily didn't see Nick or Jake until Jake walked past her and went in her kitchen door. She was starting to ask him where he was going when Nick walked up to her side and slid an arm ever so casually across her shoulder, like he belonged there, like he greeted her this way every day.

"Hey, Lily. Everything okay?" Nick asked, dropping a light kiss on her temple.

And then it was like he just took up too much space or sucked up all the air or something, because Richard backed up three steps. His stupid finger disappeared altogether, too quickly for Lily to reach out and snap it off, which she'd wanted to do ever since he stuck it in her shoulder to make a point. And then as she watched, it was like Richard just shrank or something, looking smaller and more pathetic every second.

Lily was so happy with the way Richard backed off, she forgot all about needing to take care of this herself and wanting to both scream or maybe throw something at Richard's four thousand dollars' worth of dental work or his perfect suit.

She remembered that everything had been up to her for so long and that no one had helped her with anything in months, and that she was tired and frustrated and exhausted and decided she could have reached up and kissed Nick Malone right then and there on the driveway and enjoyed it very much.

Enjoyed Richard's reaction to it, too, she thought.

But Lily resisted, settling for letting herself lean into Nick's side, like she did it every day, and smile as she said, "Just a little difference of opinion between me and Richard. He says he won't be able to take the girls for the weekend, and here they are all packed and ready to go."

"Oh," Nick said, like he belonged in this discussion, too. "Must be something really important to keep a man from being able to see his daughters. Especially this weekend."

Richard finally came out of his stupor and stopped staring at Nick and how cozy he seemed to be with Lily, and said, "Who are you exactly?"

"Nick Malone, Lily's new neighbor." He called himself a neighbor, but the hold he had on her said something else entirely.

Richard frowned and looked confused. "You didn't tell me you were seeing someone, Lily."

"Well, I didn't know you still cared, Richard," Lily said as sweetly as she could, finding a smile easy to come by in that instant, leaning against a truly gorgeous man who made her ex look as insignificant as a fussy, pouty, scrawny boy.

Richard looked even more confused then, like he couldn't

quite believe another man was attracted to Lily? Or that this particular man was?

Lily really wished she had something to throw on that suit then.

The door opened behind them, the girls walking out, and Nick let her go and moved a step away. Brittany gave her father a big hug and a pretty smile, but Ginny hung back, still cautious around him since he'd moved out.

Brittany started talking about a trip to the zoo, something Richard had promised them, and Lily wanted to strangle her ex, who looked like he wanted to strangle either Jake or Nick. She realized Nick had made sure Richard at least had to face them before disappearing on them. Either way, it was going to hurt, that he wasn't going to keep his promise to them, and Lily wasn't sure how she felt about Nick deciding to make Richard do the telling.

She started to jump in and try to explain, but Nick's hand settled against the small of her back. He leaned over and whispered, "He should at least have to face what he's doing to them, Lily."

And then Richard finally started a fumbling explanation.

Lily fumed quietly.

So he really could turn them down to their faces.

That rat!

She hadn't been sure he would be able to, but he did.

Ginny looked like she wasn't surprised and glared at her father, but Brittany started to protest.

"You promised!" she said, tears filling her pretty eyes.

Richard tried again to explain, then looked at Lily pleadingly.

Now he wanted her help?

The weasel!

But it was Nick who jumped in and saved the day.

"Lily," he said, but looked at poor Brittany. "Maybe it's better that the girls are here this weekend. I mean, I know you wanted it to be a surprise, but it is going to be Brittany's present, and this way, she can design it herself and even help us build it, if she wants. It'll be fun."

"What?" Brittany asked, eyes still watery, but perking up at the word *present*.

"You're building my daughter a present?" Richard asked.

Now she was *his* daughter.

That was great, Lily thought. Just great.

Richard didn't even remember what his own daughter wanted, Lily suspected, though she had told him, but Nick apparently knew.

"Yeah. We'll make a weekend of it," Nick said, like he couldn't wait to get started. "We'll need to come up with a design tonight and head to the home builder's store for supplies, and we'll start building first thing in the morning. What do you say, Brittany?"

"You and Jake are gonna build me a tree house?" she asked, sniffling and drying her tears.

"That's the plan. It was going to be a surprise, but maybe its better this way. Since you're going to be here," Nick said, shooting a look at Richard that had him squirming, "you can tell us exactly what you want and pick out paint colors and everything."

Lily watched as her daughter's face went from sad and stormy to happy and excited. Ginny looked relieved, Jake extremely pleased. He must have told Nick about Brittany wanting a tree house and Lily being unsure if she trusted herself to do the project.

"I want to help," Brittany told Nick.

"Okay. Let's go to the backyard and see what kind of tree we have to work with."

She put her little hand into Nick's and followed him into the backyard, Ginny and Jake going after them.

Lily just smiled up at Richard. "Well, I guess we'll see you...whenever."

He looked all put out, then practically yelled, "This is my weekend with them, after all."

"I know, but if you can't make it, you can't make it, Richard."

He threw his hands up in the air. "And exactly who is that man?"

"He told you. He's our new neighbor. Isn't he just great?"

And then Lily turned around—leaving her ex standing there fuming—and followed the weekend tree house construction crew into her backyard.

By the time Lily made it into the backyard, Nick had the kiddie construction crew organized and heading off to follow his orders.

Brittany was headed upstairs to find a book with a picture of exactly what she wanted for her tree house. Ginny was getting a tape measure from the kitchen, and Jake was headed to his house for a ladder.

Nick stood leaning against the biggest tree in her backyard, waiting, looking a little unsure of his reception.

"You mad at me?" he asked, when Lily made it to his side.

She thought about it, then admitted, "No. Not really."

"You sure?"

"Gee, Nick, why would I be mad?"

"Because I jumped into a situation that was none of my business," he said. "Gave your ex the idea there was something going on between us, when there really isn't. Made sure he had to face the girls before walking out on them this weekend, which was really not my decision to make, and then promised your daughter a tree house that you might not want her to have."

Lily nodded. "Yeah. You did. That's quite a list."

"So, I'd say you have a right to be mad." He looked a bit sheepish, as if to say he just couldn't help himself. "I just want you to know, I would have stayed out of it if he hadn't started shoving you backward with that little finger of his. Besides, it's not like I hit him or pushed him up against the side of the house or anything, and believe me, from where I stood, he deserved it and I sure wanted to give it to him."

"Okay." Lily would have freely admitted Richard poking her in the shoulder had really annoyed her. "But I could have handled him."

"I didn't say you couldn't have, Lily. I just thought…you shouldn't have to."

"Well, he's my ex. I was crazy enough at one point to trust him and marry him, to have children with him. That means I have to deal with him," she reasoned, not wanting to think about how it felt to have another man act like he had the right to protect her from the big, bad world. That was too much to think of at this moment with so many other things going on that she had to deal with.

"All right. I'm sorry," Nick said. "I have trouble standing by when a guy is manhandling a woman."

Lily wasn't sure what Richard had done would qualify as manhandling, but she let that one go.

"Tell me to stay out of it in the future, and I will," he said, sounding like he meant it. "Unless I see him put his hands on you in a way I don't like, and then you're just going to have to be mad at me. Because if I see him do that to you, I'm not walking away from it."

"Well, if that's as reasonable as you get…"

He rolled his eyes in surrender, blew out a long, slow breath and finally backed down. "Maybe we could work out a signal or something. One for me to stay the hell out of it and one that says I can do what I want with him?"

"That I'd accept," she said, laughing. "What did you say you do for a living, Nick?"

"I don't think I did."

"Mommy?" Ginny came running toward them, holding out a tape measure. "Is this what you and Nick needed?"

Lily took it from her. "Yes, sweetie. That's it."

She looked back at Nick. "I forgot the paper and the pencil. I'll go back."

And then she turned and ran back to the house before Lily could stop her. All because one take-charge-kind-of-man had taken over and started issuing orders.

Lily looked back at him and said, "Let me guess. Cop?"

"Army for a long time," he admitted. "Most recently, FBI."

"Oh." Even more dangerous than she thought. But she could see it in him. A man who didn't stand by while someone pushed a woman around, and one who was used to sticking his nose into unpleasant situations.

"I'm on leave right now, to get Jake settled," he said. "But I've worked Missing Persons in D.C. for the last three years. There are a lot of nasty people in this world, Lily."

"Richard's an insurance agent. I think by definition, they're not very dangerous."

"You never know. People you'd never think would do some-thing violent can get pushed too far, especially when strong emotions are involved—like in a divorce. And then they can do things you wouldn't believe possible."

"Then we're perfectly safe, because the only real emotion Richard seems to have left toward me or the girls is annoyance," she shot back, then immediately wished she hadn't.

Because it hurt to say it, to admit it and to have anyone else know it.

"Oh, damn," Lily said, feeling it like a fist in her midsection.

It happened like that sometimes. She could be going along, living her life, taking care of her girls, thinking they were all just fine, and then some nasty little memory popped into her mind of great times or awful ones. And then it felt like someone had shoved a fist into her belly, catching her completely un-aware, and it just hurt so bad she could hardly stand it.

She shot Nick an exasperated look and then put her back to him, wishing she could just disappear.

Chapter Six

He gave her a minute to get herself together, for which she was grateful, and she took the time to lean against the tree, fighting for a steadying breath of her own.

She was supposed to be a strong, capable woman after all.

She'd just argued that very thing to Nick, and here she was ruining it all by nearly dissolving into tears at the idea that her ex didn't give a damn about her and the girls.

"You okay?" Nick came to her side, put an arm around her shoulders.

Lily fought against that, too. Honestly, she did.

No one held her anymore. No one had in a very long time.

And it felt so good to have someone close, a grown-up, someone big and strong who wasn't depending on her to take care of him. Who actually seemed interested in taking care of her.

He would have no idea how seductive that idea was to a woman in Lily's shoes. Someone to take care of her for a change.

"You can just cry it out, if you want," he offered. "I can

handle a few tears. I mean, I don't like them, but I'm tough enough to take it. Go ahead."

Lily laughed through a shimmer of tears in her eyes and she thought she might be able to hold back now.

"You're not one of those men who just dissolves into nothing at the idea of a woman crying?"

"Now what kind of man would I be if I did that?" he said easily, still holding her pressed against his side.

Okay, Lily thought. *Just for a minute.*

She leaned into him, feeling how solid he was, how capable he seemed, how calm in the face of her little emotional storm and Richard being such a jerk.

It was like something inside of her was inching ever closer to Nick, the sweetness of him, the steadiness, the strength, the temptation of him, and she wasn't sure she had the strength to pull away.

What would be so wrong with it? she asked herself.

"Ah, Lily, I'm sorry," he said, giving her a little squeeze, his chin, his nose, then his lips nuzzling against her forehead.

Lily got herself together and backed away, shakily, but she did it.

Because of how very much she wanted to stay right there in his arms.

She shrugged, tried not to look like she'd just lost it and then had to tear herself away from him. "It just…sneaks up on me sometimes…how bad it can still feel to think of everything that's happened."

"I'm sorry, Lily. Really, I am. Especially if I made things worse by getting in the middle of it," he said, still too close for her own comfort.

She was grateful in a way for the high-handed way he'd gotten in the middle of everything with Richard, to have Richard see her as someone who'd have a new, gorgeous man by her side. And she appreciated the way Nick had stepped back immediately when he heard the girls coming. She didn't think they'd seen any of it.

But it was sheer pretense, and it needed to stay that way. Because it was dangerous to depend on anyone else but herself. Richard had taught her that very well. She no longer believed a woman could count on promises of any kind from a man.

Which made Nick Malone an obviously very nice, but very dangerous man.

Lily took one more step back to try and save herself.

"This is not your fight, Nick," she said quietly.

"I know," he agreed. "I won't do it again unless you ask me to intervene. I mean it."

"Okay." Lily nodded. "And it's really not up to you to decide whether I tell my girls their father's a jerk or he shows them that he's a jerk."

"Yeah. I know. I thought he probably wouldn't be able to look them in the eye and walk away from them today, and then I thought, if he's really going to do that, he should at least have to face them."

"He deserves that, yes, but I'm not sure if that's the best thing for my girls right now, and that's my decision to make," she insisted.

"You're right. It is. I'm sorry, Lily. The guy just really pissed me off."

"Well, join the club," she said.

She was trying to figure out where they went from here when Jake yelled from the back of the driveway, "Hey, did you mean this one?"

He was carrying a small ladder.

"No, the big one," Nick yelled back, and Jake disappeared, ladder in tow. "So," Nick said to her, "the way I see it, I have a lot to make up for. And Jake and I owe your daughter a tree house."

"No, you don't."

"Yeah, we do. I'm the one who promised her one. Oh, hell, I don't even know if you want her to have one," he admitted.

"I don't mind her having one, I'm just not sure if I trust myself to build her one that's safe."

He shrugged, grinned ever so slightly, like he knew he was pushing. "Well, then…there is something I can do to make this up to you. What do you say? We could make a project of it. You, me, the girls and Jake?"

"I'm sure you have better things to do than build a tree house this weekend," Lily said.

He shook his head. "Well, I could start going through massive amounts of paperwork having to do with my sister and her husband's estate to try to get it settled. I could try to figure out how much money's going to be left for the boys. Hopefully, they can get through college on it, but I'm not sure yet. I could start getting used to the idea that all that's left of my sister and her husband's lives is a house full of stuff, a bank account here and there, bills left to be paid, forms to fill out, a sum of some money, and three boys…. Believe me, I'd much rather build a little girl a tree house."

"Okay, but you have to let me pay you and Jake."

"No way. I'm not going to take money from you for building a tree house, especially when I'm the one who told your daughter I'd make sure she got one."

"I will pay you for your time," Lily insisted.

"How about we take it out in trade? Jake and I have had take-out three nights in a row. It's getting old really fast."

Lily knew that would make Jake happy, and she'd just double what she was making for herself and the girls. "Okay. Deal."

Lily hadn't quite known what she was getting into.

Her daughter wanted something akin to a kiddie mansion in a tree. A lavender and pink kiddie mansion.

But they soon figured out that as long as it was lavender and pink, with some scalloped trim along the roofline and a balcony, Brittany would be happy.

"Balcony?" Nick whispered in disbelief to Lily as they stood perusing shades of lavender at the paint store later that night.

"So she can play princess," Lily explained. "Little girls go through a phase where they still want to play princess on a balcony with the prince down below, begging for their hand."

Jake stood back from the overwhelming rows of paint shades, close enough to Lily and Nick to hear, and said, "You're kidding, right?"

"I wish I was," Lily admitted.

"But…like…most houses don't even have balconies, right? I mean, how's a guy supposed to do that, if the girl doesn't even have a balcony?" Jake looked really confused, then turned to Nick. "You never did the balcony thing, did you?"

"No way," Nick said.

Jake looked mightily relieved. "Whew."

Brittany came back with a paint strip with a horribly bright purple on it and held it up to Nick. "I like this one."

"Well…that's…an interesting color." Nick took it from her, then went two colors down on the paint strip, to something decidedly less bright "But the thing is, you've already picked a really bright color for the trim. The pink. And I think your mother, as a decorator, will tell you that colors with a lot of contrast look best together."

"Contest?" Brittany asked. "The colors are gonna have a contest?"

"No, contrast. More like…different. Really different," Nick tried. "And one way to make the colors really different is to use a bright color for one and a lighter color for the other. So if we did the bright pink, like this one, for the trim, we should probably go with a lighter purple. Like this."

He put Brittany's bright pink next to a lavender that was almost white, it was so light.

"See how well they go together?" he asked.

"I guess so." Brittany frowned a bit, then went back to the brighter color. "But I still like that one."

"Well, we might need a second trim color. So I guess we could get some of that, too. We'll use all three."

"Okay," she said, happy again.

Jake muttered something about girls being so weird and about being hungry. Brittany skipped the rest of the way through the home building store. Ginny kept throwing suspicious looks at Lily and Nick, like she was wondering if something was up between the two of them. Nick clearly didn't understand princess balconies or princess colors, but was obviously committed to doing what he'd promised, to build Brittany a fabulous tree house.

And Lily?

Lily was thinking stupidly that Nick was really good with her girls, much more patient than her ex, and that he was good with Jake, too, and that she was having fun in the store, buying supplies for their project, and looking forward to the weekend spent with all of them working together to build Brittany's tree house.

Like Lily was anywhere near the point of wanting another man in her life or her children's.

And then Nick Malone had to come along and build play places in pink and purple with princess balconies, even though he clearly thought it was a silly idea, just because it was what her daughter wanted.

Don't do this to me, Nick, Lily thought. *Don't.*

But he just kept right on. Charming her daughters. Guiding Jake with a blend of gentleness and firmness she couldn't help but admire, and acting like he was perfectly at home with Lily this way. Like this could be their little family, and the story had a happily-ever-after ending, and Richard and her life with him was nothing but a bad memory, fading away to almost nothing.

It was like she sat back and watched it all unfolding in front of her.

And she had a wicked craving for fudge.

Much as she tried, there was no way for Lily to hide the tree house's construction from her sister, because it was all that Brittany talked about, nonstop, all weekend, and Brittany loved to answer the phone.

So by Saturday morning, Lily found Brittany on the phone telling her aunt Marcy all about her wondrous tree house and the most wondrous tree house builders, Nick and Jake.

Marcy must have broken all landspeed records in getting to Lily's house to see the wondrous tree house builders for herself.

She found them all in the backyard, Marcy's youngest, Stacy, who was a year older than Brittany, exploding onto the scene, giggling and chattering and dancing around the base of the tree as Brittany told her all about her princess tree house.

At that point, Nick was shirtless, having worked up a manly sweat from his construction efforts, and hauling a stack of two-by-fours from the driveway into the backyard, his back thankfully to Marcy, as Marcy stood on the edge of the driveway, her mouth gaping open in a look of complete and utter awe.

"Who is that?" she finally managed to say.

"My new neighbor," Lily admitted, planting herself between Nick and Marcy, trying to have a few words with her some-times-pushy, always-talkative older sister, before Marcy charged the scene and started talking to Nick herself.

Marcy's mouth gaped open even further. "Thaaaatttt moved in next to you?"

Lily nodded.

"And you didn't tell me?" Marcy nearly yelled that.

Nick's head swung around, along with the boards, muscles rippling in his arms and shoulders from the effort in a way that had Lily going weak in the knees. Marcy might have been drooling. Lily couldn't be sure. She waved at Nick to tell him everything was fine and to go on moving what he was moving, because that would take him farther away from Marcy, at least temporarily.

"Please," Lily begged her sister. "Please, please, please do not embarrass me."

Marcy had the nerve to look offended at that.

Lily sighed and begged some more. "Please!"

"He's the Fudge Guy!" Marcy figured it out right away. "He's the reason you sounded so funny on the phone that day we were talking about fudge!"

"Yes."

"When you thought you had a fever that day, you were looking at him!"

"Yes, I was! All right! Now you know. Could we just…not do this right now in front of him?" Lily said in a furious whisper.

Marcy huffed and puffed some more, like she had reason to be offended. "And you let me think it was your hairdresser, and that you were going to do nothing but get your hair done this weekend, when this…absolutely gorgeous man is in your backyard, sweating and flexing his muscles, stripped down to nothing but his jeans and all that gorgeous man-skin. Oh, my God! Men just stop looking like that at some point, you know? I mean, I'm sure you and I can't stop traffic like we used to when we were…I don't know. A few years younger—"

"You might have stopped traffic, but I never did," Lily insisted.

"I'm not going to argue with you about that, because you've never seen yourself as you really are. But for now, my point is, men just stop looking that good when they reach a certain age, and it's just a shame, you know? Because it's really nice to look around and see really good-looking men. It's just a little perk to a woman's day to have that kind of scenery around her."

"I'm sure you look enough to know," Lily said.

"I like to look, so what? It's not a crime. I don't touch. It's nice to have something good to look at, and that man…he is worth looking at. Which you've obviously been doing and keeping it from me."

"Yes, all right? I did. I didn't tell you because—"

"Mommy, look!" Stacy called out, a look of pure glee on her face. "A princess tree house!"

"I know, sweetie," Marcy said, grinning for all she was worth as she looked from her daughter to Nick, who was bent over a board doing something, his nearly perfect backside encased in a worn pair of jeans.

Marcy just gaped for a moment.

"Mommy!" Stacy yelled impatiently.

It was all Marcy could do to tear her gaze away. "What? What, sweetie?"

"I said, I want one, too. Can I have one?"

"We'll see, Stace. We'll talk to Daddy and look at the trees in our backyard, okay?" Marcy turned back to Lily and was practically fanning herself. "Is this his line of work? Construction? Is he taking orders? Not that I'm sure I could handle having him in my backyard, looking like this. I might forget my look-but-don't-touch policy, which would be a shame, because I really do love my husband."

"I know you do. And don't worry. Nick is just doing us a favor. He doesn't work in construction. He's an FBI agent," Lily told her.

Marcy gave one of those aching sighs again, like it hurt almost, just to think of Nick, gorgeous and some kind of cool, dangerous government agent. "This man just gets better and better."

Which was the last thing Lily needed to hear or think about, because she was afraid she felt the same way. The more she saw and knew, the more she liked.

"So, why did you not tell me all this?" Marcy demanded.

"Because… I just didn't. I wasn't sure what I thought about the whole thing yet myself, and—"

"You don't know what you think about having this beautiful specimen of man living right next door to you? Lily, are you absolutely nuts?"

"No. I'm sure I have all the appropriate thoughts a woman might have when someone like him shows up next door."

"And they're all decidedly inappropriate, I hope."

"Yes, Marcy. Yes." Lily's face flamed, and she got even more flustered. "I am having decidedly inappropriate thoughts."

Marcy's lips spread into a wide, satisfied grin. "I take it he's single?"

"Yes."

Marcy's gasp was practically orgasmic.

Lily buried her face in her hands and wished she could disappear right then and there.

"Oh, honey," Marcy said. "I think this man is your reward for all you suffered through with that pig, Richard."

"My reward?"

"Yes. You don't think the universe sends us little presents from time to time? Because you've been through such a hard time, and you've worked so hard to keep the girls happy and out of the nastiness between you and Richard. You've been a great mother, but you're still a woman, and this beautiful creature is your reward."

Lily had never known the universe to offer such a reward, never imagined it delivering a man to her, to meet her womanly needs.

Oh, she thought she was a lucky woman, despite all the mess with Richard. She had her wonderful girls and a job she enjoyed and they were all healthy and happy most of the time. She had a big, loving—if nosy—family, and she thought she was blessed in many ways.

But to deliver her a man like Nick?

"Marcy, you can't possibly think the world works that way."

"Sure I can. He's here, isn't he? And looks to be the perfect...Fudge Man."

"Somebody say something about fudge?" a decidedly male voice asked.

Marcy's and Lily's heads both swung around to see Jake, a thinner, younger version of his uncle, heading from his garage to Lily's backyard, a power saw in hand.

"Lily, you're going to make more fudge?" Jake asked hopefully.

"Uh...sure, if I have everything I need, I will," she said.

Jake grinned widely. "Lily makes killer fudge."

Marcy shot Lily a knowing look. "You already made him fudge?"

"For Nick and his nephew, Jake, as a housewarming gift," Lily said, once again daring Marcy to say anything else before turning to Jake to introduce him to Marcy.

Marcy pumped Jake for as much information as she could before getting onto the subject of how Jake came to live with his uncle, and then Lily stopped her as fast as she could.

"Jake, I think your uncle needs that saw."

"Oh, sure," he said, nodding his head to Marcy. "Nice to meet you, ma'am."

"Ma'am?" Marcy said woefully. "Oh, my God, I'm getting 'ma'am-ed' by pretty boys. My life has come to this."

"You poor thing," Lily said. "Maybe you could just not talk to Jake anymore."

"Well, I had to try to find out some things. I know I can't trust you to tell me anything," Marcy reasoned.

"I will tell you that his parents were killed in a car accident two months ago, and that's why he's now living with his uncle, so try not to ask him about it, okay?"

"Oh. How awful for him. And how wonderful that the gorgeous man in your backyard is the kind of man who'd step in and raise his nephew like that," Marcy said, showing new interest in Nick.

Lily groaned.

"What? He's obviously a nice guy, not just a gorgeous one. Responsible, kind, likes kids—"

"Marcy, stop."

"Do you know how rare this is in a man?"

"I know my ex-husband hasn't been gone a year, and he didn't have all those qualities, and I'm not sure if I believe any man really does," Lily told her.

"Oh, honey." Marcy sighed and put her arm around Lily's waist. "We're just going to have to work on that, because a man like this does not come along every day."

"So, he's gone from being my gift from the universe to fulfill all my womanly needs to being family-man material in…what? Two minutes? Honestly, Marcy. Slow down. I barely know him."

"Well, you're just going to have to fix that. Women are going to be showing up in droves to snatch him right out from under your nose."

"They already are," Lily admitted. "I swear, the temperature rose ten degrees in a six-block radius the moment he moved in. You wouldn't believe how many women showed up on his doorstep bearing gifts and looking like they were dressed up for New Year's Eve or something."

"See, you have no time to lose! You have to grab this man before anyone else does."

"I don't grab," Lily insisted, as she saw Nick striding toward them, having finished whatever he'd been doing with his two-by-fours. "I'm not a man-grabber."

"Well, it's time you started," Marcy said, as Nick came to stand by Lily's side.

Lily shot her sister one more warning look, then tried to appear as composed as she could manage and said, "Nick, this is my sister, Marcy, and the little girl is her youngest, Stacy. Marcy, this is Nick."

Nick held out his hand and shook Marcy's.

Marcy managed not to melt at his feet, but just barely. "Hi," she said, a silly, breathy sound she used to make when she was sixteen and in complete awe of a boy. "I'm so glad Lily has a man next door."

She made the word *man* sound like *Greek God.*

All because he had a few muscles and a nice tan.

Lily tried to tell herself that and the fact that she was not a man-grabber. She just didn't have it in her. Never had, never would. And the competition for this man was sure to be fierce.

And yet, the man was obviously much more than a few muscles and miles of gorgeous skin.

He was a nice man.

A really nice man.

And gorgeous.

Lily couldn't deny that part.

He was building her daughter a tree house, saving Brittany's birthday weekend, and had stood up for Lily and Brittany to Lily's ex, which had been really, really nice. And he smelled really good, especially when he'd nuzzled her neck the other day.

Lily had given a great deal of thought to that neck-nuzzling, despite how hard she'd tried to forget it.

Gorgeous, nice to small children and his nephew, handy around the house, great-smelling, single and a neck-nuzzler.

Marcy was right.

Where would she ever find another man like that?

Chapter Seven

A little more than twenty-four hours later, Nick was stretched out in a surprisingly comfortable wooden chair in Lily's backyard, the masterpiece of a tree house completed.

Nick was now pleasantly sore from using muscles he hadn't used in a while, enjoying a perfect fall evening in Lily's backyard, complete with pleasantly cool temperatures, a bright, starry sky and a full moon.

The girls were playing happily in the tree house. Jake had gone to his room to play video games. Lily had grilled steaks to absolute perfection and served them for dinner.

When she showed up in the backyard a few minutes later with a small cooler with two ice-cold beers in it for Nick, he decided his life was complete at the moment.

"Lily," he said, sighing happily. "I have to say, you really know how to treat a man. And your ex has to be an idiot."

She laughed, as he'd hoped she would, and settled into the

chair beside him, holding a glass of wine for herself. "I fed you and gave you a couple of beers."

"Fed me extremely well," he corrected.

"It was a steak on the grill," she reminded him.

"Yeah. What do you think a man really wants? A hunk of red meat, a big baked potato, a few icy beers, and we're happy. Very happy. Plus, it was a great steak. What did you do to it?"

"Marinated it in some teriyaki sauce for an hour and threw it on the grill. Surely you can grill a steak."

"Not and have it turn out like that."

"So you're completely hopeless in the kitchen?"

"Yes," he admitted.

"How did you survive all these years?"

"Takeout, the deli counter at the grocery store—"

"Women to take pity on you and feed you?"

"There weren't that many women," he told her, taking a nice, cold drink of his beer.

"I have trouble believing that," she said. "Especially given your reception in this neighborhood."

"You forget, normally I would never be in a neighborhood like this."

"Okay, but still..."

Did she really want to know about him and the women he'd known? Nick supposed he should tell her, just so she knew what she was getting into.

If she was even thinking of getting into anything with him.

He was sure thinking of getting into some things with her. Maybe it was inevitable. She was right next door, right here all the time, and so appealing.

"I spent all but the last three years in the army, all over the world, really. It's not exactly the kind of life that makes for stable relationships," he told her. "I've seen more marriages break up from the stress of it all than most people have seen get started."

"It sounds like you liked the all-over-the-world part."

"Who wouldn't?" he asked, but then could see the idea didn't particularly appeal to her. "You never wanted to just get away from everything and keep on moving?"

"Every now and then, for a little while. I'd love to go to Florence and Rome for a couple of weeks. Not for my whole life."

He shrugged, then admitted, "Okay, yeah. I liked it. I liked it a lot for a long time."

"So what happened? Why'd you stop? Seen everything there was to see?"

"Maybe."

"Didn't ever find what you were looking for out there?" she tried.

"That's what my sister said," he said. "I never told her she was right. I'm not even sure myself if she was right. I just… I was ready for a change, and it was nice, the last three years to be in D.C. with the Bureau and be able to get down here to see more of her and the boys. Now that she's gone, I'm really glad we had that time. I never really understood how she did it—made a marriage work with the same man for twenty-three years—but she was a happy woman. She loved her husband, and her boys are great. She would have said she loved her life."

"And she thought your life needed to be more like hers?"

"You have a sister like that?" he asked. "Who thinks she knows everything, especially what you need?"

"You've met mine. What do you think?"

He nodded. "Yours is…interesting."

"Bossy, interfering, nosy," Lily added. "I mean, I love her, but sometimes I imagine just being able to block all her calls for a while without her just showing up on my doorstep and demanding to know what's going on with my life."

"Annie was more subtle than your sister, but she did have a way of making you understand what she thought you weren't doing what you should be doing with your life. She just kept waiting for me to…I don't know. Figure it out? She was sure I'd get tired of roaming the world one day, and I guess I did, finally. But she was still waiting for me to do…I don't know. Something different. Something more," he admitted. "And she was always trying to fix me up with women."

Lily laughed. "She didn't approve of your choices?"

"No." Nick thought about it, going back and forth with himself, thinking back through the years over the ones he'd introduced to his sister. "I mean, don't get me wrong. I like women. But they can be a lot of trouble, a lot of work."

Lily really laughed then.

"Maybe I just never found one I thought was worth all that effort."

"Ooh." Lily made a face.

"Okay, I sounded like a jerk. I didn't mean it like that, really. I've just… I've never met a woman I couldn't live without. Never met one who made me feel like it was absolutely necessary to have her in my life. That I'd be miserable without her. I'm not sure I ever will." He shrugged. "Some people just don't make those kind of connections, you know? Did you feel that way about your husband? Like he was the only one for you?"

"I thought he was in the beginning, but…maybe I just really wanted to feel that way about someone and there he was, right time, right place, right… I don't even know now."

"You must have been really young," he said.

Lily nodded. "Richard and I met in college, got married right after we graduated. We'd been together for ten years when he left."

Which had Nick wondering if maybe Richard was the only man who'd ever truly been in her life.

In her bed.

Which was a dangerously appealing thought.

It had him wondering if the man was as selfish and stupid there as he seemed to be in the rest of his life. Wondering if the man had taken as lousy care of Lily in bed as he obviously had out of it.

Which had Nick thinking about having Luscious Lily to himself, in his bed, showing her what it was like to have a man truly take care of her in bed, at least.

Would she be sweet and a little shy?

He'd bet she would.

She'd practically melted in his arms the day he'd done nothing but breathe in the scent of her and nuzzle her neck.

Ah, Lily. You're killin' me.

And then he thought, why did he have to fight so hard against this?

She was right here. He was here. They were obviously attracted to one another.

He just had to figure out how to ask for what he wanted.

Nick was up to something.

Lily knew it, and he was making her nervous.

He'd been half-naked and sweaty and grinning happily all weekend, as he worked to give her little girl a birthday weekend that was truly special.

For which Lily was grateful.

But now, it was just the two of them, Jake gone and the girls close but out of sight, playing inside the tree house.

Just her and Nick, and a dark, starlit, fall night, the man a little too close for comfort.

"So, it's been just you and the girls since your ex left?" he asked.

Lily went still. Was he asking if she'd been with anyone else since her husband walked out on her?

Surely he wasn't asking her that.

Maybe he just wanted to know that there wasn't anybody else right now. Could that be it?

Oh, he was going to ask her out!

Lily grinned like crazy, hoping the dark was enough to hide it from him.

She felt like getting up and dancing around the yard, she was so happy. Forget being so cautious and scared. Richard had been gone for more than a year, actually for a long time before that, truth be told, and her sister was probably right. She couldn't be alone forever. She had to get out there in the dating world sooner or later.

So, they'd have dinner or see a movie.

What was the big deal?

It was just a date.

"I haven't dated or anything," she said, trying for all the world to sound calm. "It took a while for everything to sink in, that Richard was really gone, and he wasn't coming back. And then there was just so much to do, to make sure the girls were okay and deal with the separation and divorce, and make sure we'd be okay financially. I haven't felt like I really had time to…do anything for myself."

He nodded, going slowly, picking his words carefully. "And, I guess it would be hard to find time to get out and meet someone with the girls to take care of."

"Yes," she agreed.

Which made it so convenient that he'd just shown up next door.

Maybe Marcy was right. He was like a little present from the universe.

Which made her think of unwrapping him very, very slowly.

Bad Lily. Very bad Lily.

"And I imagine you might not want the girls to know you were seeing anybody? I mean, that you might not know how they'd take that?"

Lily nodded. "Or worry that they might get attached to someone and then see him leave, too. Honestly, I hadn't given that much thought to the whole idea of dating. But it would be complicated with the girls."

"And for me, with Jake," he said.

"You think Jake would have a problem with you dating someone?" Lily was surprised. Jake seemed pretty reasonable.

"Oh, he wouldn't have a problem with it. He just thinks we'll have…open house, I guess you would say. I'm free to have my women sleep over, and he's free to have his do the same thing."

Lily burst out laughing, it was so ridiculous.

Nick looked pained, then shook his head and took another drink of his beer. "I think he was serious. He said it just like that. Like he didn't expect me to have any kind of problem with it. What am I supposed to do about that?"

"You're asking me? My girls are seven and nine. No one's asking me for coed sleepover privileges. And I'm very glad about that right now."

"I didn't know what to say to him. I mean, I told him he was crazy if he thought he was bringing teenage girls home for the night—"

"Good. That's exactly what you should have said."

"But what if I want to start seeing someone? Do I sneak around behind his back? That seems kind of silly, too. I mean, he's not a child, but he is only fifteen. I'm thirty-eight. Am I supposed to live like a monk or do I get some kind of pass on this?"

"I don't know if I'm the person to ask about this," Lily said. "I really don't have any experience with this kind of parenting problem. I mean, I guess you could hope to find a woman with no kids and a place of her own and make an early night of it. So Jake isn't home alone for long."

Nick grinned and put his beer down in the grass beside him, then turned to look at her. "Not gonna work. The woman I've got my eye on has two little girls."

"Oh." Lily nearly dropped her glass of wine.

Nick saved her by taking it out of her hand and putting it down in the grass, too. Then he took her chin in his hand, and very slowly, giving her time to pull away if she wanted to, leaned in close, his nose nuzzling hers, lips practically on hers.

"It's you, Lily. The woman I want is you."

Lily might have grabbed him and kissed him then.

Or he might have grabbed her and kissed her.

Actually, now that she thought about it, he wasn't a grabber.

He was exquisitely gentle and smooth and very, very sure of himself.

So it must have been her who reached out and wrapped her arms around him and hung on to him for dear life.

Anything to mean that he kept kissing her the way he was.

Warm, soft, sexy lips on hers, the heat of him seeping into her bones, his arms so strong and sure around her. Making her feel like it had been about a million years since a man had held her this way, kissed her this way, excited her this way.

She felt the same way she had when she'd looked out her kitchen window and seen him in the bright sunshine, all gleaming skin and muscles, dark golden hair and dark eyes, sexy as can be and a little bit scary.

Because it didn't feel safe to feel this way about him or any man.

But at the same time, it felt so very good.

Lily sank into him, opening herself up to him, greedy for the taste and feel of him, like a woman who'd been alone for decades.

Honestly, that's how it felt. Decades.

She clung to him, drinking in those sweet, drugging kisses of his, imagining hands all over her body, clothes stripped off, her welcoming him into her bed.

If they'd been alone, she feared that was where they'd be in five minutes flat.

The man's appeal was that potent. Either that, or she had become the proverbial sex-starved divorced woman, sleeping alone in the suburbs for way too long.

He started pulling away long before she was satisfied, his arms slowly disentangling himself from her, taking her face in his hands, his lips grinning against hers as she tried to get in one more kiss and then another and another before this was over. Like she absolutely could not get enough of him.

"Lily, honey." He laughed. "We can't do this right now. Believe me, I want to. But we can't. Jake's at my house, and your girls on the other side of the yard, and you don't want them to know anything about this. Remember?"

Lily laughed, too, because she was so happy. Because she felt alive again, after being half-dead for so long. Because a gorgeous man had moved in next door to her, and he was kind and sweet to her girls and good to his nephew, and right now, he did seem like a present from the universe, delivered right to Lily.

"Sorry. I... Oh, geez." She was embarrassed now. Happy, but embarrassed.

"I know. Believe me, I know," he said, drawing in a long breath and letting it out slowly. "At least, they have to go to sleep at some point. I don't guess you'd feel comfortable with me slipping in the back door after you get the girls to bed tonight?"

Lily still had what felt like shooting stars inside of her, felt every little zing as they zipped around inside of her, bringing her back to life.

It was like she could still feel his lips on hers, was still drowning in all the sweet sensations, so she didn't quite get what he said the first time.

"What?" she asked.

"Me, slipping in the back door after the girls go to bed tonight. You wouldn't be comfortable with that, would you?"

She looked up at him dumbly through the darkness.

All those little tingling sensations were still there, all the excitement, all the joy, but it was starting to fade and fade fast.

He expected to be in her bed tonight?

Just like that?

Lily was starting not to feel so good.

She was starting to feel foolish.

"I thought…" *Oh, no.* "You meant…when you said…and you…"

"Yeah, but I understand. I mean, I didn't think you'd be comfortable with that. What about tomorrow? While the kids are in school? It'll be just the two of us. No one ever has to know."

Lily felt like all those really good, tingly feelings drained right out of her, along with all the air in her lungs.

He wasn't asking her to go out on a date with him.

He just wanted to sleep with her.

She sat back in her chair, wishing she could disappear into the darkness.

Was this what people did these days? Just jump into bed together? Did nobody date? Maybe not. What did she know? She hadn't been single for a dozen years, after all.

Maybe she should feel flattered instead of shocked and embarrassed.

"I'm sorry," she said, just wanting to flee. "Really. I am. But, I can't—"

"Lily?"

"I just… I didn't know…uh. I have to go." She jumped up, ready to flee.

He reached for her, got a hold of her hand, but Lily pulled herself free and ran.

He called out to her as she ran, but didn't try to follow her, for which she was thankful. Lily got inside the kitchen and locked the door behind her. Which seemed ridiculous, but she did it, then put her back to the door and sank down to the floor, just wanting to hide.

It wasn't like he was going to chase her inside and demand to speak to her, or like the man was overcome with lust for her.

He'd simply…made her a proposition, she supposed. One many women might consider quite reasonable, even inviting.

One that made Lily feel like a fool.

She thought he wanted to date her, maybe romance her a bit, flirt with her, tempt her, and then after an appropriate courtship of some sort—whatever that was considered these days—she might let herself fall into bed with him.

But, no!

He just wanted her to run upstairs and take her clothes off for him.

Was that how it was done these days?

She sat there on her kitchen floor, back to the door, feeling absolutely miserable, then realized she'd left the girls in the backyard alone after dark. She stood up, unlocked the door and threw it open, to see if she could hear them playing in the tree house, and there he was, standing in the dark getting ready to knock on her door.

"Damn!" Lily cried. "I didn't want to leave the girls alone."

"They're fine," he said.

"And I just can't talk to you right now. I'm sorry. Really. I am. Please don't make me talk about it."

"I'm not going to make you do anything you don't want to do, Lily. I'm not that kind of man," he said, sounding ever so reasonable and calm.

"I know you're not. I didn't mean to imply that. I feel foolish enough as it is, and right now, I just don't want to talk about this anymore."

"Okay. How about I sit out here and keep track of your girls, so you can have some time to yourself. And when you're ready, you can call them to come inside?"

She sniffled, fighting back tears that would have made her feel even more ridiculous, and said, "That would be nice."

"Okay. I'll do that."

Try as she might, she couldn't read any kind of inflection

into his words. Not amusement, not mockery, not anything close to annoyance.

He seemed to be the most reasonable man in the world right now, which prompted her to add, "I know I'm being ridiculous. I'm sorry."

"Okay," he said.

"I just..." She took a shaky breath, and then turned her face away.

"Lily, I'm sorry I upset you. I thought we wanted the same thing, but obviously, I was wrong. I'm going to sit in the back-yard until the girls come in, and if you change your mind and want to talk to me, that's where I'll be. And if you don't ever want to talk about this again, that's fine, too. I'm sorry I offended you."

Chapter Eight

Lily stood there and watched him walk back to the yard, and then she closed her door and locked it again, just because she wanted to. Then sank back down to her floor, as hot, stupid tears rolled down her cheeks.

She was so mad at the world she could hardly stand it.

Then she grabbed the phone off the countertop beside her and called her sister.

"I am so stupid!" she announced when Marcy answered the phone.

It sounded like complete chaos in the background, which it often did at Marcy's house. Kids yelling, the dog barking, the TV going.

"John!" Marcy yelled to her husband. "Do not say another word," she told Lily. "Not until John gets here to take care of the kids and get them fed, because I want to hear every word. Every single one."

"Okay," Lily agreed, thinking to use the time to pull herself together.

"John, I have to talk to Lily. Please just take care of things for a few minutes."

Lily could hear Marcy moving through the house, probably going to hide in the garage, which she often did to get away from all the noise in her house.

"There," Marcy said, nothing but quiet in the background. "Now, tell me. What did he do? I know he did something! I knew he would! Tell me everything right this instant!"

Lily sighed, all the words getting stuck in her throat. "You don't understand. It's not good—"

"What do you mean, it's not good? I saw the way the man looked, and the way he looked at you. Of course it's good."

"I thought he was asking me out on a date," Lily admitted pitifully.

"Yes. Dates are good," Marcy said, ever cheerful. "They're a very good way to start. So? Tell me."

"He wasn't asking me out. He just wants to sneak into my house after the girls go to bed, to sneak into my bed. Tonight, hopefully. Or maybe tomorrow while the girls are in school!"

"Oh," Marcy said.

"Oh? What do you mean, oh? You don't even sound surprised. Am I not supposed to even be surprised by this? I mean, is this what dating is like these days? Someone asking if you'd like to hop into bed with them? Of course, I guess you wouldn't call that dating, would you? I'm so out of touch, I don't even know what to call it, Marcy. What do I call it? Just so I know, because apparently, this is what my life is going to be like. I should at least know what to call it!"

"Lily, honey, breathe," Marcy said. "Take a big, slow breath."

Lily, instead, tried to hold back more tears and ended up hiccupping and sniffling in Marcy's ear.

"Now, tell me again, very slowly. I mean, the man just didn't walk up to you and ask if he could let himself in the back door later, did he?"

"No," Lily admitted. "We were talking…about how hard it is to date with kids. Or I thought we were talking about how hard it is to date with kids. I guess he was talking about how hard it is to have a sex life when you have kids, and I was agreeing that…you know…it would be awkward, and that I wasn't sure if I was ready to have the girls know I was…seeing anyone. They're not even done getting used to the fact that we're divorced. And then…I don't know. I thought we were going out to dinner. He thought we were going to bed."

"Oh, honey. I'm so sorry."

"So, is this it? Am I supposed to just…go along with this or be alone forever?"

"You are not going to be alone forever," Marcy insisted.

"I don't know how to do this," Lily cried. "I just don't fit in this world anymore. I've been married forever, and I thought it was going to last forever, and it didn't, and now… I don't know what to do."

"Lily, I know it's been just rotten for you, and I'm so sorry—"

"And I didn't even want this," she complained. "I didn't go looking for it. I was fine, just fine, right here with the girls and my house and my family. I was fine! And he just showed up next door, all big and gorgeous and sweaty, making me remember all these things I didn't want to remember. Making me want things I'm scared to want! It's all so unfair, and it just makes me so mad. And I feel so ridiculous right now!"

She was crying again by the time she was done.

"I hate this," Lily said. "I just hate it!"

"I know. I'm sorry. But it's going to get better, I promise."

"How can it possibly get better? I just made an absolute fool of myself, and it's not like I can avoid the man. He lives right next door!"

"I'm sure it's not as bad as you think," Marcy reasoned.

Lily groaned. "I ran away from him. I ran inside my house and locked the door behind him and hid behind the door, so he couldn't see me. I'm sitting on my kitchen floor, behind a locked door, hiding from a grown man. It's bad. It's so ridiculously bad."

"Well, we all make mistakes…." Marcy tried.

"And he was even nice about it. I was stupid and crying and practically incoherent, and he was nice even then. He's a nice man, and even he doesn't want anything except to have a woman hop into bed with him," Lily cried.

"Honey, you're just out of practice with men, that's all—"

"Well, if this is what it's like, I don't want to practice." Practice implied doing something over and over again until she got it right, and there was no way Lily was going to do something like this again and again until she understood it and could play this game.

She had no desire to play this game.

But then…

The word *desire* stopped her right in her tracks.

Because he'd kissed her. Really and truly kissed her, and it had been…absolutely…delicious.

There was no other word that applied.

Extravagantly, wonderfully delicious.

"Wait?" said Marcy. "What was that? You must not have told me everything."

Lily sighed. "Okay…he kissed me."

"There we go." Marcy was happy now.

"And…" *Damn.* "I felt like I was sixteen years old again and had never been kissed before," Lily admitted.

"Ohh, geez," Marcy groaned. "That good?"

"Absolutely that good."

"So, then…I'm sorry, but I have to say this. What would be so wrong about thoroughly enjoying yourself with this man?"

* * *

Jake was putting Lily's lawn mower away the next weekend when he spotted Andie spying on his house once again.

At least, it looked like she was spying.

Why would she be spying on his house?

Jake pressed his back against the side of Lily's garage, nothing but half his face sticking out, so he could watch without her seeing.

Andie walked by the front of the house once, going really slowly, like she was trying to see inside the front windows or maybe around the side to the deck.

No way she was looking for him. He could hope, but he'd be wrong.

Did she really think there was something going on between his uncle and her mother? And if she did, why all the sneaking around like this? Why didn't she just ask her mother about it?

"Jake?"

He jumped at the sound of the voice off to his right, when he'd been looking left, and turned around to see Lily standing there, giving him an odd look.

"Yes?" Then he remembered Andie spying on his house, and jumped back to press his back against the inside of the garage.

"Are you okay?" Lily asked.

"Yes," he claimed. "Just… I was… I think… Andie's out there."

"Oh," Lily said, like it made sense that he'd hide in Lily's garage, rather than take a chance Andie Graham might notice him and say something to him.

Jake made a disgusted sound. "I guess that's pretty stupid, huh? Her being out there, me hiding in here. I was just…surprised."

"Believe me, I know what that's like," Lily said.

Yeah, he thought she might.

Because something was wrong with Lily, something that

started the day after they finished the tree house. Lily had made them all dinner, steaks on the grill that were fabulous, and then Jake had gone inside, leaving her and his uncle and the girls outside.

His uncle had been a bear ever since, and Lily had been... quiet and kind of sad, Jake thought.

He wanted to ask if they'd had some kind of fight, if Lily was mad, and if Jake could do anything to help, then thought of Andie spying on his house.

Was this about Andie's mom and his uncle Nick?

Was Andie looking for her mom at Jake's house? And Lily mad because she thought there was something going on between Nick and Andie's mom?

"He's not seeing Andie's mom," Jake just blurted out.

Lily looked completely taken aback, aghast and then trying to cover, failing miserably.

"Sorry," Jake said. "I thought you and my uncle had some kind of fight, and then I thought it might be about Andie's mom. But it's not. I mean, I don't know what it's about, but if it is about Andie's mom...he's not seeing her. I mean, I haven't seen her at the house or anywhere with him. Not since that first time in the kitchen.... You did know about that time in the kitchen, right?"

Lily nodded. "Thanks, Jake. But it wasn't about Andie's mom."

"Okay. Just trying to help."

"I know." Lily smiled gently at him.

"If you like, I could talk to him for you," Jake offered. "I mean, if there's anything I could do...I'd try. He's really grumpy and unhappy, if that helps."

Lily shook her head. "I don't want him to be grumpy and unhappy."

"Then you should talk to him, because he's been that way ever since Sunday night."

"Making your life miserable, is he?" Lily asked.

Jake shrugged. "He's certainly not any fun to be around like this."

"Sorry. Really, I am."

Jake glanced back outside. "There's Andie again. I don't get it. What's she doing? I mean, it looks like she's looking for her mom. That's what she was doing last time I saw her over here, but I was just at the house. Her mom's not there, and I haven't seen her mother there in weeks."

"Why don't you just go ask her?" Lily suggested.

Jake took a breath and told himself to act like a man—not like his grumpy, unhappy uncle—and just go talk to the woman.

"What do I say?" he asked, completely at a loss.

"Ask her if there's anything you can do to help her."

"Oh." That seemed simple enough. "Okay. I'll do it."

Lily laughed, looking not quite miserable for the first time in days, and wished him luck.

He walked right up to Andie, remembering at the very last second that he'd just finished mowing Lily's lawn, that he was drenched in sweat and a little grease from the mower and had yard clippings clinging to him in all sorts of places.

"Aw, hell," he muttered.

Andie whirled around, apparently close enough to hear, and looked really unhappy to see him.

Way to go, Jake.

"Hi," Jake said, because it was too late to back out now.

"Hi," she said cautiously, looking so sad.

"I was just next door, mowing the grass, and saw you walking by," he said, which he supposed made it sound like he was spying on her, which he was. But he sure didn't have to tell her that. "Are you... Do you need something? Can I help? Because, I would, if there's anything I could do."

She shrugged and shook her head. "I'm just looking for my mom."

Jake nodded.

She couldn't keep track of her mom?

What was that about?

He'd never really spent any time keeping track of his mother. It had always been the other way around—her trying to keep track of him.

"Well, I haven't seen her around here in a few weeks. And I'm pretty sure there's nothing going on between her and my uncle, if that's what you're worried about."

"I'm not worried," she insisted, though everything about her expression said she was. "I just... Sometimes she takes off and...forgets to tell me where she is, and... I just need to find her."

"Oh. Not answering her cell phone?"

Andie shook her head.

"Well, when's the last time you saw her?" Jake tried, thinking this was getting weirder and weirder.

Her mom just disappeared and left her daughter all alone and worrying about her?

"Last night," Andie whispered.

Jake was sure he'd misunderstood. "She didn't come home last night?"

Andie nodded. "Okay, you have to swear you won't tell anybody about this—"

"Sure. Okay. I swear."

"I'm not sure if she came home or not. She went out, and then I went to bed, and...uh...when I got up this morning, she wasn't there. I mean, she might have come home and gone to sleep and just gotten up early and gone out again. I'm probably being silly. I mean...she's a mother. What's she going to do? It's not like she has a curfew or friends she's not allowed to see. I just...sometimes I worry about her. That's all."

"Well, sure you do," Jake said.

He'd never really worried about his mother or father, and look what had happened to them. They'd gone out to the store and never come back. Andie's mother disappearing overnight sure sounded like reason to worry to him.

"You want to come inside, and we can talk about this and maybe figure out what to do?" he offered.

Andie hesitated. "I just really want to find my mom."

"Well, we can go inside and make sure she's not there," Jake tried.

"Okay," Andie agreed.

Lily watched from the garage as Jake talked to Andie and was happy for him when the girl followed Jake inside.

At least things were going well for someone.

She'd been steadfastly trying to avoid any contact with Nick, which was hard, and she knew she was being silly, but she still hadn't managed to make herself talk to him and try to clear the air.

She just felt so foolish and wished she could just disappear into thin air.

Honestly, to be a grown woman and feeling this way was beyond ridiculous.

She went inside, grabbed a glass of water, after working in the yard most of the afternoon, and was thinking of finding something to eat when the phone rang, and she answered it without even looking to see who was calling.

"Lily?" The voice was nothing but a whisper, but she knew who it was.

Nick.

"I'm sorry. I know you don't want to talk to me, but... I didn't know who else to call," he said, still whispering.

"What's wrong?"

"Jake has a girl here."

"I know." Lily laughed, because he sounded so flustered. Over a teenage girl? "It's Andie Graham. I saw them talking outside."

"Graham? Jake actually has Audrey Graham's daughter here?"

"Afraid so."

Nick groaned. "Is she anything like her mother?"

"I don't know. Why?"

"Because Jake brought her inside and then made up some story about wanting to show her the house."

"So? What's wrong with that?"

"Why would he care what she thinks of this house, and why would she care what the house is like?" Nick reasoned. "Come on. He's a fifteen-year-old boy. I know how they think. He walked her around the downstairs, and then they headed upstairs to the bedrooms and didn't come back down."

"Oh," Lily said. Now she got it.

"Help me," Nick growled. "What do I do?"

"You make sure the bedroom door stays open and you find excuses to walk upstairs every now and then and walk past the open doorway," Lily suggested.

"That's it? He can just waltz up to his bedroom with a girl?"

"I don't know. Can he?"

"Oh, hell, I don't know. Lily, I have no idea what to do," Nick pleaded.

Lily looked out the kitchen window, to see if she could see anything, and there was Nick, standing in his own kitchen window, staring back at her. She missed him, she realized. Missed him something fierce.

Missed even talking to him.

"Come on, Lily. It's for Jake."

"I know. I'm just not at this stage of parenting yet. Let me think," she said, trying to keep her mind on the problem at hand and not how much she missed him. "Did you ever tell Jake he can't entertain girls in his bedroom?"

"I didn't know I needed to. I mean, I told him he wasn't having girls sleep over, but we didn't exactly touch on the whole entertaining-in-the-bedroom thing. Do I have to tell him that?"

"Apparently, you do, since he's doing that right now," Lily

said. "But don't go tell him now. You'll embarrass him. Wait until she leaves, and then tell him."

"Okay, I'll wait."

"And I don't think you need to worry that much. He barely knows Andie. He was scared to even talk to her earlier, so I don't think he's going to put the moves on her the minute they get into his room."

"He's scared of her?" Nick didn't like the sound of that.

"What? You're scared of her mother," Lily said, not able to help herself from teasing him a bit.

"I am not scared of her mother. I'd just rather not have to have anything to do with her."

And then, it wasn't any fun anymore, teasing him.

It was hard, because she still felt like a fool, but she missed him, too, and she couldn't imagine it would be hard for him to find a woman to give him what Lily wouldn't.

"Audrey would let you slip in her back door after her daughter's asleep," Lily said.

Nick swore softly. "Audrey practically attacked me in my own kitchen while Jake was here. Not that it matters, because Audrey isn't the one I want."

To which, Lily had no idea what to say.

Did he expect her to believe she was the only one he wanted?

Because Lily would really love to believe that, much as it scared her at the same time.

She'd taken his offer to be nothing but the most casual of suggestions. He'd taken a look around the neighborhood and decided he'd rather have her.

But thought quite honestly that if she wasn't willing, he'd simply find someone else. All very casual and adult and not what Lily was feeling at all.

She wouldn't have been surprised to see him with Audrey Graham after that. In fact, she'd been bracing herself for that very thing to happen.

And now, he seemed to be telling her it wouldn't happen, no matter what.

"Lily, we have to talk about this. We live right next door. Jake's in and out of your house all the time, and we can't go on ignoring each other when we're living this close to each other."

"I know," she said.

"I'm sorry I hurt your feelings. It was never my intention," he said. "How about you let me deal with this girl in Jake's bedroom, and later, we'll talk."

"The girls are here," she said. "Richard backed out on them again—"

"Tonight. Will you meet me in the backyard after they go to sleep."

Backyard.

Dark.

Alone, but not quite alone.

Surely Lily wasn't afraid to meet him in the backyard.

"Okay. I'll call you when they go to sleep."

"Thank you," he said.

Chapter Nine

Like someone whose radar had picked up a signal that something was up, Lily's sister called as she was trying to get the girls ready for bed.

Lily rolled her eyes when she picked up the phone and saw who it was, then told herself not to be such a coward. How could Marcy possibly know anything?

Answer: Because she was Marcy, and Marcy just seemed to know Lily's every secret.

"So, still hiding from that gorgeous thing next door?" Marcy asked, once she'd finished complaining about what a jerk Richard was for not coming to take the girls.

"No. I talked to him today, actually."

"Oh. Good." Marcy could purr when she wanted. "And what did he have to say?"

"He couldn't really talk. He had something going on with Jake, who has a thing for Audrey Graham's daughter. And he's such a sweet kid. I'm afraid any offspring of Audrey's could eat him for lunch. Poor Jake."

"What's wrong with Jake?" Brittany said, coming out of the bathroom after brushing her teeth and getting ready for bed.

"Nothing," Lily said. "Jake's fine. Promise."

"I like Jake," Brittany said. "And he likes me."

"I know he does, honey."

"He's gonna teach me to ride his skateboard," Brittany said, her face lighting up.

"No, he's not," Lily said.

"Huh? Why not?"

"Brittany. You remember what we talked about, when Mommy's on the phone?" Lily said.

"Yes."

"Well," Lily held up the phone, so her daughter couldn't miss it, "Mommy's on the phone."

Brittany pouted, but got into her bed. "I need to know how to skateboard."

"Not tonight, you don't. We'll talk about it tomorrow." Lily kissed her daughter on the forehead and walked out, leaving the bedroom door cracked open. "Sorry," she told Marcy.

"It's okay."

"We should be good to talk now. Ginny's already in bed, reading. She probably won't move for hours."

"Good. And I don't really care about poor Jake's love life. I care about yours and your lack of any kind of life at all. What's going on with you and the gorgeous one?"

"He wants to talk," Lily admitted.

"Okay. When?"

"Tonight. Outside in the backyard."

"In the dark?" Marcy's grin came through the phone as easily as her words.

"Yes, it's getting dark," Lily admitted.

"Okay, just please, please, please, think about this before

you turn the man down flat. Because I know you like him, and I know he's gorgeous—and also nice—not an easy combination to find in a man. And he wants you. So what if it's just sex? I mean, the man can even do home repairs—"

"I can do most any home repair," Lily said, hardly able to believe she was having this particular conversation. "You're not really going to tell me I should sleep with a man to get a leaky faucet fixed, are you?"

"No, I'm saying you should sleep with him because the last man you slept with was your jerk of a husband who left you feeling lousy about yourself and men in general. And that you've been alone a long time, and I understand that you're scared to get involved with someone again and to trust anyone. Really, I do. But that doesn't mean you have to be all alone right now."

"I'm fine with being alone," Lily insisted, walking into her own bedroom and shutting the door, so the girls wouldn't hear any of this conversation.

"Of course, you are. I didn't say you had to have a man," Marcy reasoned. "I was just saying…why not let yourself have this man. Just because… Well, just because. Why not?"

"Maybe because my life is complicated enough—"

"Complicated? Your life is lonely. Your life is full of kids and your house and me. You can have more than that. I am here to tell you that you deserve more than that," Marcy said.

"But I'm not ready to get involved with anybody. It's way too soon."

"Perfect. The man doesn't want to start anything serious. He just wants to have sex, and I'm just guessing here, but I bet he's really good at it."

"Oh, just by looking at him, you figured that out?"

"No, by watching him build that tree house. He's careful and strong and so sure of himself. He's patient and kind. I heard the way he talked to the girls and was letting them help, and you said he's so good with his nephew—"

"That's how you judge how a man will be in bed? By how he is with kids?" Lily was highly skeptical.

"That's how you judge how a man is at his core. If he's that way in real life, he'll be that way in bed."

Okay, Lily had to admit, there was probably something to Marcy's reasoning. She'd certainly imagined herself that he'd be kind and considerate and patient and...thorough. Lily imagined him being very thorough. *With her.*

"The question to ask yourself, honey, is why not? Why would you not simply enjoy what this beautiful man has to offer? He's already said you two can keep it quiet and private, so no one needs to know. It'll be your little secret. And mine, of course."

Lily rolled her eyes. Of course, her sister would want all the details.

"Think of it as part of the reclaiming-yourself-as-a-woman, post-divorce-recovery effort," Marcy suggested.

"We're making a recovery effort now? That makes me sound like a disaster area, and believe me, I've felt like one, but I didn't imagine someone making a formal declaration. My life as a disaster area."

"You need to know that not all men are jerks, and that you are a young, sexy, desirable woman, and that you will have a life again, and this man is ready to remind you of all that."

Lily frowned.

Marcy made it sound so easy.

And so appealing.

"I guess... I'm just afraid," she said.

"Of course you are. You got flattened by life, by a man you trusted who was supposed to be with you forever. But you're not dead, honey, and it's time to start remembering that," Marcy said. "Are the girls down for the night?"

"I think so."

"Then go call that man."

BUSINESS REPLY MAIL

FIRST-CLASS MAIL   PERMIT NO. 717   BUFFALO, NY

POSTAGE WILL BE PAID BY ADDRESSEE

SILHOUETTE READER SERVICE
3010 WALDEN AVE
PO BOX 1867
BUFFALO NY 14240-9952

Get FREE BOOKS and a FREE GIFT when you play the...

LAS VEGAS

GAME

Just scratch off the gold box with a coin. Then check below to see the gifts you get!

YES! I have scratched off the gold box. Please send me my **2 FREE BOOKS** and **FREE GIFT** for which I qualify. I understand that I am under no obligation to purchase any books as explained on the back of this card.

▼ DETACH AND MAIL CARD TODAY! ▼

335 SDL EVA7   235 SDL EVF7

FIRST NAME   LAST NAME

ADDRESS

APT.#   CITY

STATE/PROV.   ZIP/POSTAL CODE   (S-SE-01/09)

7	7	7	Worth TWO FREE BOOKS plus 2 FREE Gifts!
🍒	🍒	🍒	Worth TWO FREE BOOKS!
🔔	🔔	♣	TRY AGAIN!

www.eHarlequin.com

Offer limited to one per household and not valid to current subscribers of Silhouette Special Edition® books. All orders subject to approval.

* * *

Nick was literally pacing back and forth in the living room, willing Lily to call, when Jake came downstairs and found him.

"Is something wrong?" Jake asked.

"No," Nick lied.

"Because, you look like something's wrong."

Nick took a breath and wondered how much to tell the kid. "Just waiting for a phone call."

"Oh."

Jake hesitated, looking unsure of himself. "Did something happen?"

"No," Nick said. "Why?"

Jake shrugged, looking really young and maybe even scared. "Just…wondering."

"Nothing bad happened, Jake," he said, because Jake seemed to be waiting for the next bad thing to hit, something Nick forgot at times. "Sorry I worried you."

Jake shrugged. "I'm gonna warm up some spaghetti from last night. Want some?"

"No, I'm good," Nick said, then figured he really should talk to the kid about the girl and his bedroom being off-limits.

He followed Jake into the kitchen and tried to remember how his father would have handled something like this. He probably would have just barked out an order. *No girls in your bedroom!* And Nick would have said, *Yes, sir,* and left it at that.

Not that he hadn't managed to sneak a few in.

Something he really liked thinking about now that he was the parent, at least temporarily, and was supposed to keep that from happening.

"Jake, about you and Mrs. Graham's daughter…" he began.

"Yeah?" He'd been inspecting the contents of the refrigerator and didn't even lift his head.

"She's…uh… She looks a lot older than you are."

"Only a year and a half," Jake admitted, pulling out a plastic container of spaghetti leftovers.

"She's...are you two... I didn't know you were seeing anyone."

Jake laughed. "I'm not. She just...she's having some trouble with some stuff and needed to talk. That's all."

"Oh." That was a relief.

"Of course, I would love to do much more than talk to her. I mean.... She's hot. Don't you think?"

"I think a man my age could practically get arrested for even thinking that, so I'm going to pass on that question," Nick said.

"You don't think she's hot?" Jake was incredulous.

Nick thought she was enough to scare the parents of a teenage boy half to death, to blank out all reason in the adolescent mind, which was already not that high in the ability-to-reason area, especially when anything female was within reach.

"I think you really don't need to be entertaining girls in your bedroom, okay?"

"Entertaining?" Jake laughed. "We were talking."

"Fine. Talk in the living room. Or the kitchen. Or outside. Not upstairs," Nick told him, because a door cracked open and Nick pacing back and forth outside just didn't seem safe enough.

"Okay," Jake said. "No girls in my bedroom."

"Okay. Good," Nick said.

That settled that.

No argument. No harsh words. No big deal.

Good.

So why did Nick still felt like he was standing in a minefield, Jake and all these girls, all the possibilities for trouble.

Parenting, he decided, was terrifying.

Lily finally worked up her nerve and made the call, then realized it had started to rain while she'd been worrying and talking to Marcy.

Darn.

The backyard, while offering enough privacy to get into trouble, still seemed much safer than having him in her house.

Which was silly, Lily knew, but…she was looking for any sense of safety she could find, and she was pretty sure the man wouldn't seduce her in the Adirondack chairs in her backyard.

Her kitchen was another thing all together.

Nick answered the phone, that deep, smooth tone of his enough to make her want him, despite how uneasy she was with the whole idea of letting another man into either her life or her bed.

"It's raining," she said.

"I know. Is that a problem?"

"Well, I don't know."

"Are you scared to let me in your house, Lily?"

He didn't say it in a teasing, flirty way, just completely matter-of-factly.

"No. I just… I don't know how to do this," she confessed. "I've been alone a long time. I feel like I've been alone forever, and at the same time, I feel like I've been married forever, and I don't even remember how all this works."

"I know," he said, softly as could be, a world of understanding there.

Marcy was right. He was patient and kind and gorgeous, and Lily would bet money all that came into play in making him great in bed.

"And I'm tempted. Very tempted—"

"I'm glad to hear it," he said, chuckling.

"But it's just not as simple as that. Not for me."

"Okay. I think I knew that all along, Lily, but you can't blame a guy for hoping. So, what do you want to do? Pretend this never happened? Because if that's what you want, I'll do it."

"What if I don't really know what I want?" she asked.

"Well, that could lead to all sorts of things," he said, sounding much more pleased with himself or her or maybe just the moment. "It could lead to me giving you some time to figure out what you want. Me trying to convince you that you want the same thing I do, which I am perfectly willing to do. In fact, I think that could be a lot of fun. Let me try to talk you into it—"

"Talk me into it? Because I didn't think you were talking about a conversation."

"Talking would be part of it," he insisted, sounding like he planned on doing very little talking.

And the other part?

Lily had a feeling she'd really like the other part.

She stood at the window, looking out through the darkness and the rain, trying to see past it all to him.

He was grinning. She could hear it in his voice, and he was so cute when he grinned. It took all that toughness out of his face and made him look instead like a big, sweet, sexy man.

"I think you should let me come over and kiss you good-night," he said. "To give you something to think about."

Lily shook her head. "I have plenty to think about, and I'm not sure you coming over here is a good idea."

"It's a great idea. We'll stay in the kitchen. How much trouble could we get into in your kitchen, with your girls upstairs and Jake over here, used to waltzing in and out of your house all the time? Besides, it's just a kiss, Lily."

Oh, but she'd been kissed by him before.

"Hang up the phone," he said. "I'll be there in a second."

The phone clicked, connection broken, before she could protest.

She'd hardly had a chance to take a breath when he was there, opening the back door and letting himself in.

The rain must have picked up, because it was dripping off his dark, thick hair, had left wet splotches on his shirt, and the look in his eyes when he watched her was enough to make her sizzle.

His charm was a potent thing.

"Let me dry you off," she said, reaching for a clean dish towel from the drawer beside her.

She reached up to press the cloth against the side of his face first and then his forehead, his other cheek, his lips, the touch somehow becoming more of a caress than anything else.

Lily caught her breath, not thinking until then that to take care of him in this way, she had to get very, very close to him. His hands came up to hold her loosely against him, the warmth of his big palms soaking into her back, making her want to do nothing but lean in even closer to him.

She tried to concentrate on the task she'd set for herself, moving onto his hair and then somehow it was her hands, not the towel, brushing the water from the dark strands.

"I've never had anyone dry me off before." He grinned wickedly, not pulling her closer, but making no move to step back. "You're making me wish I'd stayed out in the rain a while longer. If I'd known I was going to get this kind of treatment, I would have."

Lily dropped the towel on the floor, embarrassed by what she'd done, not sure if it was a way to stall what he'd come here to do or just an excuse to touch him, which she found herself wanting very badly to do.

And now, he was here, her in his arms, her with nothing at all to say and nowhere else she wanted to be.

He went still and quiet, his body all but surrounding hers, until he seemed to take over her senses. She could feel the heat coming off of his big body, feel both the patience and the urgency inside of him, and the self-control. She could smell his slightly minty aftershave and hear his slow, even breaths, could feel his chest rise and fall with each one, could swear she felt him staring down at her.

Ever so slowly, he bent his head down to hers, doing nothing more than laying the side of his face against hers.

Lily closed her eyes. Her hands latched on to his arms and held him there almost against her, but not quite.

Don't go.

Don't come any closer.

She wanted both things very much.

His breath warmed her ear for a second before he whispered, "You can have as much time as you need to get used to this, Lily."

"I don't think I could ever get used to anything that feels this good," she admitted.

He laughed against her ear, and then he kissed the side of her face, her jaw, her neck, like a man who had an eternity to do nothing but tease her.

She shivered at each touch. Her nipples bunched into hard peaks, her breasts trembling and seeming to know they were inches away from being nestled against his chest, and she could hardly breathe.

He was grinning. She could tell as his mouth closed against the point where her neck smoothed out into her shoulder, and it was like a jolt went right through her at the contact.

She wrapped her arms tight around him as her whole body sagged and he caught her close, holding her there, letting her feel just how different they were. His body was big and unyielding, even more solid than she'd imagined, made of the kind of muscles that had been tried and tested over a lifetime of what had obviously been very physical work, and she wanted to touch him everywhere.

He was done teasing.

He picked her up easily, as if she weighed next to nothing, and backed her onto the kitchen countertop until she was sitting there, his body nudging her legs apart, sinking in between them.

His lips found hers, and she opened herself up to him, to the heat of his mouth and the delights of his hands running up and down her back.

Lily groaned and wrapped her arms around his broad chest,

thinking this was what a man was supposed to feel like. This was how a woman was supposed to feel in the arms of a man.

Tempted and turned on and all tangled up inside of him and what he was doing to her.

She just opened herself up to him and let him take what he wanted, let him kiss her again and again and again.

He groaned deep in his chest. His hands slid down to cup her bottom, and then he pulled her up against him and leaned into her. If they both hadn't had clothes on, he'd have been inside of her.

As it was, she felt everything he had to offer her, wrapped her legs around his waist and rubbed herself up against him, aching for him, just like that.

He hesitated for the first time, pulling away from her lips just enough to mutter, "Damn, Lily. You're about to make me forget everything I promised you when I came over here tonight."

Which let her know she wasn't the only one who was so turned on she could hardly stand it.

Lily arched herself up against him once more, feeling that big, throbbing hardness against the place in her that ached. He caught her bottom in his hands and held her there and groaned again, his face pressed against hers once more.

"I thought we'd be safe in the kitchen," he said, still holding her there, shaking his head back and forth, breathing hard. "Apparently, I was wrong."

"Apparently."

"Just stay right here and let me enjoy this for a minute before I make myself let you go, okay?"

And it was still there, all the heat, all the longing, all the possibilities, stretched out between them, holding them there like an invisible bond.

It was delicious and thrilling and so tempting.

"You could kiss me again," Lily said shamelessly, lifting her face to his so he could do just that.

"No, I couldn't," he said, easing her back down onto the

countertop and pushing her face down to his chest. "Tell me to go. Tell me to go right now."

But Lily didn't want him to go, especially now that she knew how safe and yet how turned on she felt in his arms.

She eased back and lifted her face to his. "But I don't want you to go."

He shot her a look that told her she was in very dangerous territory. "Don't you do that to me—"

"Do what?"

"Look like you'd give me anything I wanted right now, but you trust me not to take it."

"I do trust you not to do anything else."

"That is so not fair. Not after you caught fire in my arms."

"Okay, it's not fair."

"And you don't look like you're the least bit sorry," he teased.

"I'm not," she said and reached up to kiss him again.

He let her have one kiss, but carefully held his body away from hers.

"I'm leaving," he said. "And if you invite me into this house at any point when the girls aren't here, you'll be naked. I'm just telling you so you know that. Unless it's what you want, we should not be alone here together."

"Okay," she said, thinking that was in all likelihood completely true.

"Think about what you want, Lily. Be sure."

"I will," she promised.

"I have to go."

He kissed her once more, kissed her hard and quite thoroughly, and then he was gone.

Lily lay in her bed that night, unable to go to sleep, and kept running through those moments in the kitchen with him.

Those delicious kisses, the hardness of his body, the gentleness of his touch. It was like she'd been asleep for what felt like decades, and he'd come along and awakened every bit of sexual feeling inside of her, and she wasn't quite sure what to do about that.

Tearing off his clothes came to mind.

But then she had to consider taking off her own clothes, which made her think of her thighs, which she hated most any time she really looked at them.

And then she thought of those last six months or so with Richard, the halfhearted lovemaking that hadn't been love at all on Richard's part, just guilt and obligation and probably trying to keep Lily from getting too suspicious about what he was doing with someone else.

The humiliation she'd felt upon finding out.

The vow she'd taken to never trust another man again.

The fear she felt at the idea of doing just that.

And then she came back to having to take off her clothes in front of another man for the first time.

Complete and total darkness seemed to be a good idea, but then she'd really like to see Nick naked.

Maybe she could be in the dark, and he could be in the light. No, she could undress him in the light and admire him there, and then pull him into the darkness and shed her clothes there.

Yeah. That could work.

Problem solved.

Maybe she could dream of him, have him there in her dreams, find some satisfaction in the fantasy of him without ever really having to trust him enough and take the risk of really letting him into her life, even if it was just sex.

Could she make that work?

Erotic dreams of Nick?

If she was lucky, Lily decided.

If she was very lucky, Nick the Dream-Lover would be enough.

Chapter Ten

She slept fitfully all week and without an appearance by Nick in her dreams.

That Friday, thoroughly disgusted that her dream plan hadn't worked, she concentrated on getting cranky, sleepy girls ready for school and out the door, then what she had to do with her own day.

The girls were anything but cooperative. Brittany couldn't find her favorite red shirt and didn't want to wear anything else. If Ginny weren't only nine, Lily would swear her daughter had PMS and was trying to get on Lily's last nerve by objecting to anything and everything Lily said that morning, even the most normal and reasonable of requests. If this was what lay ahead for Lily, parenting preteen daughters, she was truly frightened.

Richard called to whine about this and that—as if Lily still cared—but it was really to try to explain how he could take the girls on Sunday that week, but not on Saturday and how difficult and stressful and challenging his life was. Lily managed not to reach through the phone and smack him, but just barely.

She needed to go shopping, because she had to make cookies for a party of some kind for one of Brittany's classmates the next day, and Ginny was complaining that her shoes hurt her feet, which meant she'd probably outgrown another pair. One more thing for Lily to take care of.

But first, she had to get some work done in the dining room. The wooden trim had been there, waiting for her to put it up for days, and Lily tried. Honestly, she did. She'd finally decided on some fancy, arts-and-craft wooden trim, actually more like small panels, that she was assembling in the garage. A million little pieces, it looked like at the moment. Impossibly time-consuming, but also ridiculously popular right now.

So she tried.

And got nothing but a huge splinter in her palm, but she persevered beyond that.

It was when she smashed her thumb being careless and distracted with her hammer that she really got mad.

"Ahhh!" She actually yelled, because it hurt and she was so frustrated.

She threw the hammer down in a rather unladylike fit, and it banged against the concrete floor of the garage and maybe bounced off the opposite wall, probably putting a gash into the wall that Lily would have to fix later.

But she didn't care at the moment.

She grabbed her throbbing thumb to try to stop it from hurting and when that didn't work, stuck it in her mouth and sucked on it.

Nick found her like that, sucking her own thumb and near tears. He must have heard her yell or heard the hammer bouncing around in the garage.

He came to an abrupt stop, seeing that she was relatively okay, and stood there, maybe scared to come any closer.

"Don't worry, I won't throw anything at you," she said.

"Promise?" he asked, mouth twitching, like he was trying not to laugh.

"Well, if you start laughing at me, I might!"

And then he did burst out laughing.

Lily, much to her own horror, burst into tears right there in her garage.

Nick looked horrified. "Lily, honey. I'm sorry. I didn't realize you were really hurt."

He rushed to her side and started running his hands over her arms, looking for a broken bone or something.

"I'm not hurt," she said, sniffling furiously. "Just my thumb. I smashed my stupid thumb with the hammer. I'm just…"

"Yes?" he asked, seeming genuinely concerned.

"I'm just mad!" she said, giving up on maintaining any dignity in the situation at all.

He looked flabbergasted and unsure for a moment, maybe afraid of a woman who was all over the place emotionally, then rallied and scooped her up in his arms. "Come on. Let's get you inside and get some ice on that thumb."

Lily gave up and let him carry her, which wasn't any kind of hardship at all, really. She even let her head rest against his chest, took deep, shuddering breaths and tried to stop crying before she really freaked him out.

He got her into her kitchen and sat her on the countertop, then found a dish towel and wrapped ice in it. He came to stand in front of her, as he'd been that night they'd kissed with such abandon, right here in her kitchen, took her hand in his and gently wrapped the towel around her poor thumb, then held it there with his own two hands.

"Better?" he asked very gently.

Lily nodded, still able to feel the tears falling down her cheeks.

"Bad day, Lily?"

"Yes," she whispered.

"Bad week?"

"Yes."

He winked at her. "You're not quite as tough as you look, are you?"

She brought her chin up at that.

"No, don't take it like that. I didn't mean it like that. It's just that…you seem like you can do anything. Like you're Super Woman. Jake thinks you absolutely walk on water. You make all this parenting stuff look effortless. Like you know exactly what to do and how to do it, and you don't need help from anybody. But some of that's just an act, isn't it?"

"It's all an act," she admitted. "I'm never sure of the right thing to do, and I'm tired all the time and mad and…lonely. I'm really lonely sometimes."

There, she'd said the hardest thing.

"Especially since you moved in next door," she added, then immediately felt guilty for it. "Okay, no. That's not right, either. It's been nice having you and Jake there. Really nice. But…it makes me miss things, too."

That looked like it interested him quite a bit.

"What kind of things?" he whispered.

"You know. A man. I miss…having a man in my life, and I didn't before, or maybe I just didn't notice. I don't know. But now, I do."

He nodded, considered, then said, "Sorry."

She frowned. "You are not. You want things from me, and you make me want…all those things, too. And things were much simpler when I didn't want those things. I wish I just didn't want all those things."

He shrugged, as if he just couldn't help himself. "Jake and I could pack up and move, if it helped."

Which made Lily laugh a bit.

She knew she was being foolish, and she knew that he knew it, too.

And he didn't have to be so nice about it or so charming or so close.

"I felt safer when you weren't here," she admitted. "Safer not wanting the things you make me want."

"Could we expand a little on what exactly you want and maybe on why you can't let yourself have it?" he tried.

"Because… Well, I'm not sure why right now. Because I'm scared. The last year was awful, and I'm just starting to feel safe again, and I don't want to get hurt. Again."

"Okay." He nodded. "I can understand that. But…you're lonely, too. You're a beautiful, young, sexy woman, and you're lonely. You're allowed to do something about that, if you want, aren't you?"

"I don't know. It's never really seemed that simple to me. I have the girls and all these things to do, and I'm so busy, and… I really don't like my thighs," she blurted out.

Nick's lips really twitched at that one. "How is that even possible, Lily?"

"No woman really likes her thighs!"

"But I've seen yours. I've seen them in those cute little shorts you wear when it's really hot outside."

"I don't wear little shorts," she insisted.

"I'd be happy if they were even littler, but the ones you have are really nice. Trust me. And I liked what I saw."

Which was nice to hear.

Still… "And…I'd have to take my clothes off if we were to….you know."

Nick considered for a moment. "You want me to say you can keep your clothes on? Because if that's what it takes, honey, I'm willing. I mean, I'd prefer that you take them all off, but if you insist."

"Well…maybe if it was really dark…." Lily conceded.

"Really dark and you keep your clothes on?"

"No. I mean...I don't know! I did think... I was kind of hoping... I really want to see you," she confessed. "All of you."

He laughed out loud then. "Lily, honey. I would do anything I could to make you comfortable with this, and I am absolutely willing to take off every stitch of clothing I have on, and you can keep most of yours on, if you must. But I just don't see how this can work if I'm in the light and you're in absolute darkness."

"I know, I'm being ridiculous! Believe me, I know."

"I mean, we really have to be in the same room, and I don't get how to make half of it light and half of it dark—"

"Stop it!" she cried. "I already feel foolish enough."

He grabbed her and wrapped his arms around her, laughing as he did it, and she reached out and wrapped her arms around him, too, her poor thumb forgotten along with her towel and her ice.

It fell to the floor, the ice clattering and skating along the floor, as Nick leaned down and kissed her, finally, and she forgot how foolish she felt and all her doubts and most of her fears, and she remembered, completely, how wonderful it was to have a big, strong, sexy man in her arms.

At the moment, it seemed impossible that she'd been without one for so long, because suddenly, it was like she couldn't stand to go another minute without this.

She kissed him back with a fury, wrapped her legs around him and pulled him to her.

He groaned and palmed her hips and pressed her against him, and she felt his body's growing response to hers.

It was like going from zero to sixty in seconds flat, and it left her thinking she could just tear his clothes off of him right there in her kitchen.

Which to Lily was nothing more than a fleeting thought, but to her surprise and shock and absolute pleasure, he pulled his shirt over his head and threw it in the direction of the dining room, and then she had a beautifully shirtless man, miles of honey-brown skin and smooth muscles, in her arms.

Lily shuddered and debated the wisdom of exploring all that beautiful skin with her hands and her mouth versus the idea of begging him to carry her upstairs right then or maybe just into the living room and onto the sofa.

It was such a difficult decision to make.

Especially since he was still kissing her like a man literally starving to death and every now and then gently thrusting against her open thighs, a tiny, increasingly frustrating version of what she really wanted him to do.

He finally dragged his mouth back from hers long enough to whisper, "So...exactly where would you like to see me naked, Lily? And when were you thinking of this happening? Please tell me you were thinking right now. Because I think now would be a really good time."

She ran her hands down the smooth, broad plane of his back, enjoying herself all the way, then came to the waist of his jeans, slid down and cupped his hips, pulling him to her.

He groaned, his forehead falling until it rested against hers.

She looked at him, then looked at his gorgeous body, followed that swirl of hair on his chest as it narrowed into a thin line down the center and then disappeared beneath his jeans.

She reached out and kissed one side of his chest and then the other, and one of her palms started slipping down, following that line of dark hair.

His whole body stiffened. He gave her a look that said she was heading into dangerous territory and she'd better know what she was asking for before she did it, but Lily was beyond doubts now.

She let her hand slip down over the waistband of his jeans to find an altogether impressive bulge and cupped him with her palm. She was looking right at him as she did it, so she saw his eyes go even smokier and narrow in on her face like he couldn't see anything but her. He sucked in a breath and stood there and let her explore as she wished, rubbing him and then slipping her hand down inside his jeans.

He sagged against her, his forehead to hers as he half gasped, half laughed, and she thought about how much she wanted him inside of her, right then, big and hot and throbbing.

"Okay," she said. "If you have a condom, I'll get naked."

"Right, front pocket," he whispered.

"You carry a condom around with you?" She was happy, mostly, but surprised.

"Since that last night with you in your kitchen, I do. It seemed like a really good idea," he said, kissing her neck, taking his teeth to it gently, then not so gently as she gasped.

He started to undo her jeans, and she protested, "Someone might see us, Nick."

He turned and looked out her kitchen window. "Only if they're snooping around between the side of my house and the side of yours."

And then he waited, hands on her waist. She closed her eyes and said, "Okay. Let's live dangerously."

He grinned, undid her jeans and then somehow lifted her with one arm and pulled them and her panties off with the other. Lily peeled her T-shirt off while he pushed down his jeans and put on the condom.

He looked back up at her, then the bra, then her again, waiting.

"In my kitchen?" she protested.

He nodded, took her mouth. "Yes, Lily, right here in your kitchen. We'll do it in the dark, behind a locked door in a bedroom next time, I promise."

Which was an image that pleased her almost as much as it shocked her to be naked in her kitchen, but naked she was as she peeled off her bra and threw it in the direction of the sink.

He gave her a purely wicked grin, then hauled her up against him, so her breasts nestled against his chest. She closed her eyes and thought of that day he moved in, all those pretty muscles and the hot skin, standing here in her kitchen practically panting over just the idea of him and how long it had been since she'd even noticed a man in that way and how long it had been since anyone had touched her.

And now, here he was, naked in her arms and as beautiful as ever, even more so, she decided.

He was kissing her relentlessly, like he could devour her whole, and gently rocking against her, giving her a moment to get used to the feel of him and to make sure she was ready for this. Lily already knew she was, embarrassingly so.

He palmed her hips, his big hands hot and insistent, pulling her to him, thrust once easily, then again.

Lily groaned.

"Too fast?" he asked.

"No, not fast enough," she told him, feeling downright greedy for him.

And then he slid all the way inside.

"Ahhh!" Lily nearly yelled, because some things just felt too good. Too impossibly good.

He held her there, firmly but gently, rocking ever so slowly against her, which only multiplied sensation on top of glorious sensation.

The man felt impossibly good there in her arms.

Her breath came in little pants, and she was afraid there were tears seeping out of the corners of her eyes, that her whole body was awash in sensations and emotions of every possible sort, and it was all just overwhelming at the moment.

His hands still cupped her hips, fingers digging into them as he tried to control his movements and hers.

"Lily," he warned, because she couldn't be still, couldn't stand it, or maybe she couldn't move slowly enough, or maybe it was just his way of tormenting her and driving her crazy, and she was messing with his concentration or his self-control or something.

But it turned into a battle of sheer will, his versus hers, to see who could drive each other over the edge first.

She used the muscles in her thighs to thrust herself against him and kissed him hard and ran her hands all over him, very, very glad that he had taken all his clothes off in the light.

"You are so bad," he told her, when she refused to be still and let him set the pace.

She grinned up at him.

He kissed her hard, thrusting and thrusting against her, until everything in Lily's body went impossibly tense and then just stayed there, frozen in time and space with him, before she tumbled over the edge.

Wave after wave of pure satisfaction echoed through her. She cried a bit more and buried her head against his neck, felt him pulsing deep inside of her, shuddering, gasping for breath, gasping her name.

"Lily, Lily, Lily."

They stayed right there, clinging to each other.

Lily was suddenly exhausted, her legs aching, her arms clinging to him even harder, tears still flowing.

He held her tight, so strong and yet so gentle, his chest heaving against hers, making her want to do nothing but burrow closer and wishing they were somewhere in the privacy of a deep, dark place.

But they weren't, and he was trying to figure out what was wrong, trying to see her face, dry her tears.

"Hey," he said. "What is it?"

"Just… I don't know. My eyes are leaking."

"Leaking?"

"Yes, leaking," she insisted.

He gave her a little grin.

"They just do that sometimes," she said. "I'm not upset. I'm not crying. I'm just… My eyes are leaking. Don't you ever get…overwhelmed and find that your eyes are leaking?"

He shook his head.

"Well, mine do," she said, feeling overwhelmed, still, and a bit shy and extremely naked. "Can we go hide in the dark now?"

"Sure. Just give me a second."

He turned away from her, but stayed close enough that she didn't fall off her perch on the countertop, got rid of the condom and pulled up his pants. Then he lifted her into his arms and carried her upstairs to her bedroom.

She snuggled against his chest and closed her eyes, trying not to think of the fact that she'd just had sex with him in her kitchen in broad daylight and that she had few, if any, regrets about it, except for being embarrassed for behaving so shamelessly and not getting her way about doing it in the dark.

Not that being able to see him didn't have its definite advantages.

She directed him to the door on the right, and he got her on the bed, tucked under the covers, then bent over and kissed her.

She wrapped her arms around him when he went to pull away, afraid he might disappear, that this might have all been a dream. Nick, her Dream-Lover. That was easier to believe than them getting naked in her kitchen.

He grinned down at her, letting her hang on to him, but said, "I need to run over to my house and grab something."

"Another condom?"

He nodded.

"Feeling pretty sure of yourself? That you'll be needing it?"

"Hoping. Just hoping. And not wanting to be caught unprepared."

"There's a box of them in my bathroom. Far right drawer, buried in the back," Lily admitted. "My sister gave them to me after she got a look at you."

He grinned and headed for the bathroom. "Remind me to thank your sister the next time she comes to visit."

"That is not funny," Lily yelled after him. "Don't you dare, Nick! Don't you dare!"

* * *

She found he dared most anything.

He walked back into her bedroom like a man who felt very much at home there, closed the blinds tight, asking if that met with her approval and her need for sheer darkness.

"It's better," she said.

Then with the bedside light still on, he watched her as she watched him slowly, matter-of-factly, strip for her once again.

Lily blushed, couldn't help herself.

He was an absolutely beautiful man.

All tanned skin and hard muscles everywhere, a hard stamp of satisfaction in his smoky-dark eyes.

And he wanted her again.

His body left no question about that.

Her breath started coming fast and shallow, and she itched to touch him all over.

"Seen enough?" he asked after a moment.

"No," she said.

"Hey, I'd be happy to leave the light on. I'm just trying to give you what you want, Lily."

She shot him a look of exasperation, because the man knew he'd already given her exactly what she wanted and more, and he was about to do it all over again, and he knew that, too.

Wanting to put him a little off balance, too, if she could, Lily slid over in the bed to his side, reached out to turn off the light herself and then in the darkness, found one, well-muscled thigh with her palm, finding heat and firmness to the touch, a bit of roughness from the dark hairs there.

He let out a breath, but didn't say anything else.

She pressed the tip of her nose against that thigh, running up and down the muscle there, then nibbled a bit, taking in the scent of him and liking it.

"Lily," he groaned.

"What?"

She got up on her knees on the edge of the bed, and wrapped her arms around his waist, her breasts against his thighs, kissing his chest and then letting her head fall back for his kiss.

He lifted her right off the bed and wrapped her legs around him once more, squeezing her hips, rubbing up against her.

"I don't seem to have the patience to do this right today," he said, kneeling with her on the bed, laying her back against it and then following her down, his body hot and hard on top of hers. "Sorry."

"Sorry?" she got out between long, deep, thrusting kisses.

"We'll do better next time," he said, like a promise.

Lily let her thighs fall apart, giving him her body to do with as he pleased, and a moment later, he was inside her once again, and it was even better this time, if that was possible.

She loved having the weight of him on top of her, the sheer volume of the man, those broad shoulders and the tight, sexy hips, all those beautiful muscles flexing and straining, propelling him up and back and then down and in once again.

Lily clung to him as best she could, content to let him set the pace, to let him take what he demanded. She started whimpering when it all got to be too much, clutched at his shoulders, might have sunk her nails into his back in protest when she didn't think she could take it anymore.

And then she gave up, gave up all sense of self-control or pretense or self-protection, and just let herself be with him, be his, be completely free and it was like everything fell away. Like nothing else mattered or even existed, except being there with him, and she was nothing but sheer feeling, sheer pleasure.

He groaned on top of her, gave one more, deep, long thrust, and she felt a pulsing deep inside, first from him and then her own, and then she just didn't care about anything at all, except how good she felt.

* * *

He crushed her to him, breathing hard, lying heavily on top of her, waiting for the sensations to end, trying to hang on to every last second of bliss. Lily would have held him, too, if she'd had the strength. As it was, it was all she could do to lie there, her arms falling to her sides, breathing heavily, limp as could be.

Nick nuzzled the side of her neck, her ear, her cheek, his breath still harsh and heavy.

Ever so carefully, he rolled to his side, waited there for a moment, then rose from the bed and made his way into the bathroom. He was back a moment later, getting in beside her and then pulling her to him, until she rested against his side, his arm thrown casually around her, her face against his chest.

He kissed her forehead and told her to rest, and then the world fell completely away.

Chapter Eleven

Lily woke to a languid warmth and pleasant near-exhaustion that made no sense at all.

She was so relaxed, she thought she might have taken a pill of some sort. A fabulous pill, if it could do this to a woman.

She rolled over in her bed, her skin feeling so good against the soft sheets, feeling tingly and alive, like every pore was happy.

Since when were her pores happy?

"Lily?" She heard a deep, husky voice and felt a slightly raspy cheek press against the side of her face, warm breath on her ear, tickling it. "What time do the girls get home?"

"Girls?"

She had to be dreaming.

She never felt this good awake.

Then she remembered wishing for her Dream-Lover, Nick, thinking she could make do with nothing but the dream, and then remembered the reality of Nick, the lover, insistent and demanding and so maddeningly sure of himself and what he wanted and how to get it.

She remembered her kitchen.

Where he'd gotten it.

She'd left her clothes there, she feared.

"Oh, my God!" Her eyes flew open, searching for the lighted digits of her alarm clock. "Three-ten?"

Lily shrieked, planned to throw back the covers and jump out of her bed, but then realized she was naked.

Nick sat there. "Three-ten is bad?"

Her mouth hung open for a moment, then she waited, fearing the sound of a door opening or footsteps on the stairs. Hearing none, she looked at Nick and demanded, "Go downstairs and get my clothes! Hurry!"

He didn't argue, threw back the covers and went.

Naked.

Really cute, but naked.

Lily whimpered.

He stopped in the doorway, came back and grabbed his jeans off the floor and yanked them on, heading out the door as he fastened them.

Lily grabbed underwear from her top drawer and yesterday's jeans and a T-shirt from the top of the clothes hamper in her bathroom and dragged everything on as fast as she could.

She straightened her bed and then ran down the stairs, worried that Nick might have trouble finding all her things. She had no idea where they'd ended up, just remembered flinging her bra in the direction of the sink.

The door opened just as she got to the bottom of the stairs, the girls blowing into the room like a happy, chatty storm, hardly paying her any attention to her at all, except to call out a greeting.

They dropped backpacks and kicked off shoes into their favorite corner of the room and headed for the kitchen.

"Girls!" Lily called after them, managing to get them to stop and turn around and look at her.

"Mom, are you okay?" Ginny asked, looking at Lily like she was a puzzle Ginny would figure out if she tried hard enough.

"Of course, why?"

"You look funny," Ginny said suspiciously. "Your hair's all messed up."

Lily smoothed down her hair as best she could, wishing she'd taken a moment to look in the mirror, then smiled nervously and claimed, "I was working hard all day."

Then Nick stepped out into the hallway leading to the kitchen, his hair messed up, too, but fully clothed, thank goodness.

He looked like he had no idea what to do, having been caught in her house as the girls came home.

Had he found her underwear, at least?

Lily tried to mouth, "Underwear?" at him.

"What?" Ginny asked, definitely knowing something was up now.

Nick shook his head and frowned at Lily.

Did that mean he hadn't found her underwear, or that he didn't know what she'd tried to ask him?

She didn't know.

And it didn't look like she had time to find out. She just shooed him away as best she could by nodding toward the door behind him, and then giving him a little wave with her hand that she hoped said clearly, "Get out now!"

"Mommy?" Brittany said, coming to hold the hand that Lily was waving, maybe like a woman in the midst of a seizure.

"I'm fine, honey, just…starving. I'm starving," Lily claimed, realizing it was true.

She'd slept through lunch and burned off a bunch of calories in the kitchen and in bed.

How could she have done that in her own kitchen?

She'd never be able to go into that room again and not think of what she and Nick had done there.

And she sure wasn't going into that kitchen now.

"I'm hungry, too," Brittany said.

"Me, too," Ginny added.

"Great. How about we go out for pizza?" Lily suggested.

She could get her girls to forget anything by offering to take them to their favorite pizza place. It was a treat she saved for moments when it was absolutely necessary to distract them from something.

Did that make her a bad mother?

She hoped it didn't, but at the moment she was just grateful to understand so fully how to manipulate her girls.

They scrambled back into their shoes and headed out the door, Lily bringing up the rear.

Whew.

She was safe, for the moment.

Now all she had to do was get the girls upstairs when she got back home and search the kitchen herself.

And try not to think about what she'd been doing all day with Nick.

Lily got through an early dinner with the girls just fine, and then managed to shoo them off upstairs when they got home.

She was frantically searching her kitchen and trying to call Nick a moment later when her back door opened and in walked her sister.

"What is the matter with you today?" Marcy asked as she came barreling into the room, her youngest daughter, Stacy, behind her.

Lily froze, thinking to herself, *What is the matter with you, Lily?*

Years of careful living, gone out the window, lost on the

kitchen countertop, and she still didn't know where her underwear was.

Maybe Nick had found it and taken it with him.

An idea that Lily kind of liked, when she thought about it, then imagined seeing her pretty pink bra in those big, strong hands of his, maybe shoved into his front pocket to remind him of what they had done.

Her face turned bright red, she was sure, and she turned away to try to hide it, went to the sink and turned on the cold water to try to cool herself down, wishing she could immerse more than her hands into the cool spray.

She feared she absolutely reeked of really good sex.

The girls wouldn't know what it was, but Marcy would.

"I...I'm sorry," Lily said. "What did I do?"

"You forgot me, Aunt Lily," Stacy cried, bottom lip trembling visibly when Lily turned around to look.

"Oh, no!" Lily said, not remembering until that very moment. "Oh, honey, I'm so sorry. You were supposed to come here after school today, weren't you?"

Stacy nodded, looking like she'd been orphaned for life, instead of forgotten about for an afternoon playdate while her mom went to the dentist.

"I had to go home with Angelica instead, and I don't like her," Stacy said, laying on the guilt. "And her mother said you were irr...irrreee."

"Irresponsible?" Lily guessed.

Stacy nodded.

"She's right. I am so sorry, Stacy. I just completely forgot. I was working on the wooden trim for the dining room, and then I... I guess I just lost track of time completely, and then the girls and I went out for pizza."

"Pizza?" she said wistfully.

Lily had just made it worse.

"Aunt Lily will find a way to make it up to you later, Stacy," Marcy said. "For now, why don't you go upstairs and play with Brittany?"

"Okay," Stacy said, shooting Lily a look that said she would definitely expect to have this made up to her in spectacular fashion.

Lily had finished with her hands and was drying them, paying extraordinary attention to getting them perfectly dry, and wondering if that slight burn in her cheeks meant she'd been roughed up a bit by Nick's afternoon stubble and if he might have even left a mark on her neck.

Tons of possible things that Marcy could see and then know…

But it seemed Marcy didn't need to see or maybe she already had or maybe she just knew, because Lily's sister looked absolutely delighted.

"Lily, sweetie, what did you do all afternoon?" Marcy asked with a twinkle in her eyes.

"Nothing," Lily insisted. "I mean, I worked. I had a lot of work to do."

"I bet it was more like…somebody worked you over," Marcy said.

Thoroughly, Lily thought, trying so hard not to let it show in her face.

"He finally gotcha, didn't he?" Marcy asked, grinning from ear to ear.

"Marcy, I… Honestly—"

Marcy walked toward her, like she was going to corner her or something. Lily tried to dodge her, thinking to slip past the refrigerator and into the hall. She could run, if she had to.

"I just forgot about Stacy. I'm so sorry. But it's really nothing—"

And then Marcy reached behind Lily and up, above Lily's head, and pulled Lily's favorite pink bra from… Must have been from the top of the refrigerator.

"Been looking for this?" Marcy asked, the pink lace dangling from her hand.

Lily grabbed it and went to put it in her pocket, but she didn't have one, so she settled for hiding it in a drawer behind her.

"He got your bra off in your kitchen?" Marcy asked, laughing.

"He got everything he wanted in this kitchen," Lily said, suddenly deciding to come clean and get it over with. Marcy would probably get it all out of her eventually anyway.

She had the satisfaction of seeing Marcy's look of complete disbelief at first.

Lily glared back at her sister, not backing down one bit from that statement.

"No way," Marcy said.

"Fine. Don't believe me. He didn't get anything."

"No, wait," Marcy insisted. "Wait. I want to know. I won't argue one bit. I just…need to know, okay? I'm your sister, and I've been sleeping with the same man for twenty years, Lily. I need to live vicariously for a moment and I got a look at him, so I can guess that he's really, really good at…everything. So, please, do me this one favor and tell me everything!"

Lily's cheeks flamed as she thought of being here in this room with Nick, how crazy and out of control it had been, how it had been completely unlike anything she'd imagined letting herself do with him.

Marcy groaned, like Lily thought she must have done when Nick sank his teeth into her neck and took a little bite of her.

"That good?" Marcy asked.

Lily nodded, simply having no words.

Marcy sank back against the counter like she'd just been reduced to a puddle, which was how Lily felt, too, every time the man so much as looked at her.

"Well," Marcy said. "If it couldn't be me with that gorgeous hunk of man, I'm glad it was you, honey. You deserve it."

"I have no idea how to handle a relationship like this," Lily said. "I mean, do I even call it a relationship?"

"Beats me," Marcy said.

"What do people call it these days?"

"I have no idea. I could ask my next-door neighbor. She has kids in their twenties. She'd probably know."

"And where do we go from here? What do we do?"

"Anything you two want," Marcy said. "But wait, before we forget, did you ever find your panties? Or should we be looking for them before the girls come downstairs?"

"What did you do today?" Jake asked that night as he and Nick ate take-out Chinese.

Nick tried to look completely innocent and asked, "What do you mean?"

Jake shoved a huge forkful into his mouth and halfway chewed before saying, "You seem…I don't know…happy or something."

"What am I, a grump, normally?"

Jake shrugged. "Not really, I guess. I mean… You just seem awfully happy."

Nick shoveled the last of the kung-pow chicken onto his plate before Jake, the human garbage disposal, could get to it, and lied through his teeth, "I didn't do anything, really. I mean, it was a nice day out. Sunny…and…nice."

Jake looked at him like he didn't believe a word of it.

Nick touched a hand to the outside of his jeans over the pocket where Lily's little pink panties were, for safe keeping until he could return them. He'd shoved her shirt and jeans into the cabinet above her refrigerator, along with her bra, thinking her girls wouldn't be able to reach that spot and would never find them.

But he'd had trouble finding the panties and then the girls had come in, and he didn't think he had any choice, really, but to take them with him.

They were still there, still tucked safely away from sight,

making him a little crazy for her every time he remembered they were there.

Lily, turning into a beautiful, half-wild woman in her own kitchen.

He would never have guessed that.

"See, there," Jake said. "You do look happy."

Nick tried his best to look grumpy and told Jake he needed to take out the garbage and clean up his room. Jake just shrugged, as if he was not fooled at all, and got up and took his plate and glass to the sink to rinse them off, then put them in the dishwasher.

Nick fought the urge to pick up the phone and call Lily, fought an even stronger one to wait until Jake was upstairs for the night and Lily's girls were asleep, to slip across the side yard and into her house and return her panties.

If he was really lucky, to carry her off to bed again.

He didn't think she'd go for that with the girls home, but a guy could give it his best shot and see what he could get before she kicked him out for the night.

His phone rang as Jake was collecting his backpack to go upstairs and do his homework.

Nick grabbed for it with unseemly haste, which also caught Jake's attention, and said, "Hello," probably sounding happy just saying the word, thinking it might be Lily.

"Nick, I finally caught you," a distinctly unhappy voice said.

"Hello, Joan."

Jake made a face. Joan was his father's older sister, the relative who made the most vocal objections to Nick getting custody of the boys and a real pain in the ass.

"If I didn't know better, I'd think you were dodging my calls," she said, in a tone that made it sound like she'd actually said, *You jerk, quit dodging my calls.*

"Jake is just fine," Nick said as pleasantly as he could manage. "In fact, he's right here—"

Jake was shaking his head like a madman, mouthing vile threats toward his uncle if Nick dared give the phone to him.

"I didn't call to talk to Jake. I called to talk to you," Joan said.

Nick mouthed to Jake, *Fine, you're off the hook. Now get upstairs.* Then turned around and tried to find some patience to deal with Joan.

"You're still determined to be responsible for these boys?" Joan asked him.

"Nothing's changed, Joan. We're still here. We're still fine. There's nothing for you to take care of," Nick insisted, wondering how his sister stood having this woman as an in-law.

He knew Joan made her a little crazy, but lately he wondered how they'd never come to blows. Joan was…pushy would be the nicest Nick could imagine. She thought she knew everything, including all there was to know about raising teenage boys successfully.

Jake ran from her when he saw her coming and thought her kids were freakishly perfect on the outside and a complete mess on the inside. Nick thought Jake might be right.

He felt like he could see her glaring at him through the phone.

"Fine. Take your six months, although I doubt it will require that long for you to see what a mistake this is," she said. "I'm calling about Thanksgiving. I think it's very important that the boys be with their family this year, of all times, and I thought I might cook dinner and serve it in their house, so they could have one more Thanksgiving at home."

Nick's first thought was that he'd rather eat in front of the TV, watching a football game, and suspected Jake would be fine with that. Jake's father would have been fine with that, too. Nick had spent Thanksgiving at their house, doing just that, until his sister dragged them all away from the TV long enough to serve dinner in the big dining room.

Joan would have pitched a fit, but his sister had lived in a house full of men and understood. They'd eat, digest awhile in front of more football games on TV, and then move into the backyard for a vicious game of football of their own.

It was relaxed and raucous and just about time being spent together as a family.

"Well?" Joan asked, pushy as ever.

"I'll think about it," Nick said. "And I'll ask the boys what they want to do. We'll get back to you."

He got off the phone as fast as he could, swore long and loud in a way he tried not to do in front of Jake, but when he turned around, Jake was still standing there behind Nick, looking worried.

"She's still trying to get you to give up custody, isn't she?" Jake asked.

"No," Nick said, finding a feeling of satisfaction from seeing that Jake really did want to stay with him. He was never sure how things were going, still wasn't sure he could do this and do it right. "Joan just wants us to spend Thanksgiving with her."

"Ooh! No," Jake said. "She'd have a fit if we wanted to watch a game."

Nick shrugged. "I'll try to be a bit more diplomatic than that when I turn her down."

"You know, I was thinking maybe we could spend it with Lily. You think she'll ask us?"

"I don't know. She may have plans with her family. Her sister's house is only about thirty minutes from here."

"I bet Lily makes a killer Thanksgiving dinner."

Which had Nick picturing her in the kitchen.

Which led to him picturing other things.

Things he shouldn't be picturing with Jake in the room.

"You have work to do," Nick said. "Go."

And Jake went.

* * *

Nick paid some bills, did some paperwork and watched Lily's house as one-by-one the lights went out, then saw her walk into the kitchen.

So, she'd gotten the girls to sleep.

Then he walked across the side yard and knocked on her door.

She stared at him through the glass door for a moment before opening it, looking very pretty and hesitant and a little embarrassed.

"I wasn't sure you were going to let me in," he said.

Her cheeks took on a pink tinge and she looked away, biting her lip not to say anything.

Nick laughed softly, feeling like in this moment his life was as close to blissful as it had ever been. He was surprised he even recognized the feeling.

Digging a hand into his front pocket, he tugged on pink lace until a bit of it showed. "I got everything else in the cabinet above the refrigerator—"

"No, you got my shirt and my jeans in the cabinet. The bra didn't quite make it. It was lying on top of the refrigerator. Mostly on top, I should say. My sister found it."

"Oh." Nick nodded. "Sorry. I thought I got it all in there. I tried. Really, but it all happened so fast."

Was she mad or just embarrassed?

He couldn't quite tell.

"I was going to do my best not to tell Marcy anything, but with the bra as evidence, I didn't stand a chance against her," Lily said. "You've met her. You know what I was up against."

She still wasn't looking at him, and he wasn't going to let her get away with that all night. He took a step closer, planting himself right in front of her, backing her up against that spot on the counter with two hands at her side, holding her loosely, not touching her with anything but his hands, but needing to know.

"Are you mad, Lily?"

"No," she said, staring at the floor.

"Do you think I pushed you into doing something you weren't ready for?"

"No."

"Something you didn't want?"

Her gaze came up to his then. "From what happened here, I don't think there's any room for doubt about me wanting you."

Yes.

He'd needed her to say it.

He knew. No question from the way she'd caught fire in his arms. But he'd needed it spoken out loud between them.

"And what do you want now?" he asked, because just as much, he needed to know where they went from here.

"My girls are upstairs," she said.

"I know. But they won't always be here," he said, watching her breathe in and out, watching the space between them and knowing how easy it would be to erase it completely, wanting to sink into her all over again, thinking she really was the most amazing woman.

All quiet and comfort and gentleness on the outside, as much toughness as she needed to handle whatever life threw her on the inside, and a sweet, innocent, eager sexiness that had blown him away.

He couldn't wait for the girls to leave again.

"No, they won't always be here," she said.

"But I could be. Anytime you'll let me. On any kind of terms you want."

She laughed, sounding a bit nervous. "I just give you a little sign—" She raised a finger and motioned him closer. "And that's it?"

"That's the signal?" He nodded. "Then I'll be here."

"Well, that's handy. A man at my beck and call."

He laughed out loud then.

Lily shushed him with her fingers pressed to his lips. "The girls might still be awake, and I don't want them to know about this."

"Okay. Sorry," he said. "Now kiss me, and I'll give you your panties back."

Lily wrapped her arms around him and pulled him close, into a soft, devastatingly inviting, womanly embrace, opened herself up to him and gave herself to him as sweetly and eagerly as she had that morning.

He pulled away long moments later with a groan, pulled her panties out of his pocket and gave them to her and left, thinking he would sleep deeply, satisfyingly, and dream of her.

Chapter Twelve

Dreaming of her was not enough, Nick discovered.

And the next day was Saturday, and her ex backed out on taking the girls again, that rat. He did take them on Sunday, but Jake just always seemed to be underfoot.

So Nick had to wait until he watched her get the girls off to school Monday morning, watched Jake leave, had some coffee and then waited some more, trying not to seem as desperate for her as he felt.

He made it twenty minutes before he showed up next door to find her painting fancy wooden trim to use on her walls.

She just looked at him, a paintbrush in her hand, a bit of white paint on her nose, and said, "I don't recall giving you the signal."

"Well, I was afraid I might have missed it, being next door," he claimed.

"So you came over just to be sure you hadn't missed it?"

He nodded. "And then...I had an idea."

"Nick, I have to get some work done."

"I know. But I'm not bad with a hammer. I mean, I built that great tree house in the backyard. I was thinking, I could help you with your work. With two of us, we'd get it done in half the time, and that would free up some time in the afternoon for…whatever you want."

"For whatever I want? It's what I want?"

"I was hoping we'd want the same thing," he admitted.

And they did.

He knew it.

"You think I'm going to spend every afternoon in bed with you?" she asked, like it was ridiculous to even think that.

"I can hope, can't I?"

She laughed as he came closer, held him off with her wet paintbrush, and said, "Well, I'm going to have to see how productive you can make these mornings. Because, if you think you're going to come over here and make me forget all about how much I have to do—"

He got her then, grabbed the paintbrush with one hand and her with the other arm, pulling her close, holding her weapon carefully out of reach.

"Nick—"

"Don't make me use this," he threatened, pointing the brush at her.

"I mean it. I have to work." She tried pushing him away, but didn't get very far with that. He had her, and he wasn't letting go just yet. "I have to fix up this house and sell it and make some money, so I can feed my growing girls—"

"Make me a deal, Lily."

"Make you a deal? I have to bargain for—"

"Time, honey. We're negotiating about how we're going to allocate our time to accomplish the things we both want during the day, since we don't have our nights free."

"You make it sound so reasonable," she said.

"I'm a reasonable man," he claimed.

She laughed once again, and he got her close enough to kiss her soundly and then had to remind himself they were in her garage and the garage doors were open, and it was not quite ten o'clock in the morning.

"All right," she said when he got done kissing her for the moment. "We'll make a deal."

"Good. What do you need to get done today?"

She gave him her list, and he said, "Okay. Once we do that, the rest of the day is ours. Deal?"

"Deal."

He'd have her in bed by twelve-thirty, and the girls didn't get home until three. Nick thought this would be the beginning of a thoroughly satisfying way to spend their days.

Lily's life had taken a turn toward decadence.

She spent a few hours a day working on her house with Nick and a few hours most every day in bed with him.

She'd sneaked into the lingerie shop one morning after driving the girls to school and bought a big bag full of new undies. When Nick found out what she'd done, he'd tried to get her to promise to let him go to the store with her next time, so he could help her make her selections. No way she could walk into a lingerie store with him.

Then he started sending her undies in the mail in plain brown paper packages.

She blushed all the way to the mailbox, and all the way back, and was sure her neighbors knew something was going on, watching her the whole time she was retrieving her mail, wondering what she could possibly be getting in those plain, brown paper packages.

He made it a game, to see how quickly he could convince her to abandon her work plans and get her into bed, and they always ended up skipping lunch, so they were starving by the time the girls got home. Lily had taken to making a meal at three o'clock, which puzzled both the girls and Jake, but no one objected to eating it. And then she fed the girls and herself a snack at eight o'clock or so, which, again, they didn't really understand but didn't object to, either.

Richard asked her something about moving mealtimes, and she thought about the look on his face if she confessed, "I've taken a lover, and I just can't get myself out of bed long enough to have lunch, which throws my whole schedule off."

She wished she had the nerve, but evidently, the look on her face said enough.

"Are you seeing someone?" he'd asked, the girls loaded into the car for one of those rare times when he actually kept his scheduled visit with him.

"I see a lot of people," she claimed, then to herself added, *But I'm only having mad, passionate sex with one man, and he is soooo not you.*

She went to the neighborhood association meeting, where different groups planned activities throughout the year and was bombarded with questions about Nick and wild speculation about his love life, and she just smiled and claimed not to know a thing. Except that he was the nicest man, and so was Jake.

And she couldn't walk through the neighborhood grocery store without someone telling her he was surely going at it hot and heavy with Audrey Graham.

Poor Audrey.

Lily honestly felt sorry for her, missing out on the wonder that was Nick Malone.

She didn't think she'd ever had a more delicious secret in her whole life or a more pleasure-filled time. A part of her knew there was no way it could go on being so good for any length of time. She knew he had serious reservations about his abilities to be the parent Jake needed now, and that Jake had an aunt, Joan, who was even more convinced that Nick was not the man to be the boys' guardian. She knew he missed his job in Washington, D.C. She knew that he saw this time as something he owed his sister, to see how things worked out between him and Jake, and that even if he did keep Jake in the end, that didn't mean he'd be here or that he'd be with Lily.

She knew all those things, and yet another part of her was falling hard for him, wanting everything he'd been so careful to never promise her, everything he'd never wanted from a woman.

But she tried hard not to think of that, tried to stay in the moment, especially the ones when they were alone.

Weeks passed.

Halloween came and went. She dressed up as a seventies flower child in some things she picked up at a thrift store, and when Brittany told Nick if he wanted to go trick-or-treating with them, he had to dress up, he pulled out a beautiful dark suit, a pair of dark sunglasses, clipped his shiny shield to his breast pocket and told Brittany he was going as an FBI agent.

Brittany didn't think much of the costume until he pulled a pair of handcuffs out of his pocket.

He managed to convince Lily to let him chain her to her own bed the next day by telling her she didn't have the guts to do it, then took complete advantage of her.

Thanksgiving was fast approaching. The twins were coming home from college. Jake was excited to see his brothers. Nick could not imagine the commotion, the sheer volume of noise that would be made or food consumed in a house with three adolescent boys, and Lily was thinking she'd have to do without having him alone for five whole days, which seemed like an eternity to her now.

How had she ever lived this long without him in her life?

He was nothing like Richard in bed.

Even in the early, heady days with Richard, it hadn't been anything like this.

Nick was demanding, patient when it really counted, impatient at times and that worked, as well, paid such attention to the finest details, took note of everything she liked and exactly how she liked it, and taught her exactly what he wanted from her and when, could be adventurous and fun or exercise the kind of self-control that drove her mad.

She felt sorry for every woman in the world who would never have him as a lover, but she wasn't about to share.

She found herself lying in bed with him one rainy afternoon in November, a chill in the air outside, but toasty and warm, curled up against him, thinking he was the most beautiful man.

He was sprawled out on his stomach in her bed, sleepy and satisfied, and she was curled up against his side, her head on his shoulder. She peeled back the covers a little bit at a time, running her hands over every bit of skin she revealed, her fingers making little patterns on his shoulders, his back, kissing her way down his spine.

He laughed deep in his throat.

"Lily?"

"Hmm?" she said, her hand slipping under the covers to cup that sexy bottom of his.

"I thought you were too tired for this."

"I'm just touching you," she said, thinking about the way he looked in those faded, worn jeans of his, about the play of muscles in his hips when he was on top of her and inside of her, how she liked to have her hands here on his bottom when he was deep inside of her.

She leaned over and kissed the base of his spine, and felt his body slowly come to life, desire streaming through him like a golden light, heat following, breath quickening, heart thudding.

Even knowing what it was like, probably exactly what he was going to do, knowing how it felt, how he smelled, how he tasted, how hard and harsh his voice could get when he was really close to the edge of his self-control, even then, she still couldn't wait to have him, to be in his arms, skin to skin, opening herself up to him, holding nothing back.

She couldn't wait.

And she couldn't seem to get enough.

"You're going to cripple me one of these days," he said, slowly rolling over, grabbing a condom and then pulling her on top of him.

Lily grinned.

She liked it this way, liked it every way, truth be told, but really liked it this way because of the way he watched her. She settled herself on top of him, close, but not taking him inside yet. She leaned down to brush her hair against his chest, brush a kiss against his lips and then her breasts against his chest. And then she rocked against him, still not taking him.

And all the while, he watched her, telling her how it felt when she did this or that, telling her how sexy she was, how pretty, how much of a tease.

After a while, he'd take a handful of her hair and pull her to him, take her hips in his palms and maneuver his way inside of her, and then let her do what she wanted for another period of time, fighting for control, while she tried to tear that control of his to shreds.

And then he'd take her by the hips once again and pull her into the rhythm he wanted, sometimes letting her stay on top, sometimes not.

It didn't matter.

What did, was that she got to be with him, tease him, kiss him, torment him, end up spent and barely able to breathe, weak and boneless, wrapped up in his big, strong arms.

She felt so safe in his arms.

That day, she teased him for as long as she could, felt his hands on her hips as he slowed the rhythm down, until he barely let her move at all, so that the slightest movement at all felt like so much more. She dug her fingernails into his shoulders, tightened every muscle in her body around him, felt his hands dig into the flesh of her bottom, holding her still, right there on the edge.

Until they both just shattered, everything falling away.

She cried out his name, saw that hard, satisfied smile come across his face, and then she collapsed in his arms.

They stayed that way for a long time.

His hand stroked through her hair. He kissed her lips once, then again, then rolled her onto her side and disappeared for a moment, coming back a moment later to pull her back to him, spooning against her, his front to her back, his arms wrapped around her, her cheek pillowed on his arm, his lips kissing her cheek, then toying with her ear.

She was sure she'd never get enough of him.

Jake opened the door one afternoon in November and found Andie's mother standing there, giving him a bright smile that somehow seemed odd.

"Mrs. Graham," he said. "Hi."

Standing in the doorway, teetering on ridiculously high heels, wearing a tight, short black skirt and a low-cut top, she struck a pose that seemed as if she were offering her breasts up for his viewing pleasure. He tried not to look.

"Hi," she said, kind of purring in a way. She brushed past him and into the living room, uninvited. "Do me a favor, honey. Tell Phillip I'm here."

Jake stood there. "Phillip? Who's Phillip?"

She laughed, her voice all throaty and inviting. "You know. Phillip. He isn't expecting me, but he's always glad to see me."

Jake closed the door and then followed her through the downstairs as she called out to someone named Phillip.

"Mrs. Graham, I think you have the wrong house," he said, though honestly, how was that possible?

She'd been here three or four times flirting with his uncle. How she could not remember who Jake was and who his uncle was and that this was their house?

She headed for the stairs, missed the second step and started to fall. Jake caught her and then eased her down to sit on the step. And caught a whiff of her breath in the process.

She'd been drinking.

At four in the afternoon?

He tried to keep her where she was, not wanting her trying the stairs again, but she didn't like that.

"I'm fine," she insisted. "And I'm not leaving until I get to see him."

"Okay," Jake said. "He's not here, but I can call him and maybe he'll come home."

That seemed like the best thing to do.

Except he'd call Andie.

He didn't think her mother would know the difference, at least not until Andie got here.

Jake reached for the phone. He knew Andie's home number because he'd thought about calling it a million times, but chickened out. He thought of the two times she'd been here, looking for her mother, and wondered if this was the problem—that her mother drank and wandered off or got lost or something.

Andie answered on the first ring, sounding anxious as she said, "Hello."

"Andie? It's Jake. Jake Elliott."

"Who?"

"Your neighbor. Two streets over. I go to your school," he said, trying to ignore his own humiliation at being completely invisible to her.

"Oh. Yeah. I can't talk right now. I'm really busy. Sorry," she said, then hung up on him before he could say anything else.

"Great," Jake muttered, disconnecting the call, then hitting redial.

"Look," she said when she answered. "I told you, I have something I have to take care of. I can't talk to you now. Goodbye."

Jake swore and hung up.

Maybe he could get her mother home by himself. If she'd go willingly…

Then he realized he'd lost her.

"Mrs. Graham?" he called out, searching the downstairs for her.

He found her in the kitchen with a bottle of Scotch that his uncle kept in the back corner of the pantry. It tasted absolutely vile. Jake knew because he'd sniffed, then taken a sip and nearly gagged. How could anybody drink that stuff?

Mrs. Graham found a glass and poured herself a drink.

"I don't think you need that right now."

Jake went to get the bottle away from her, but she wouldn't give it up, and in the process, the Scotch in the glass sloshed out and ended up mostly all over Jake's shirt. She dropped the glass, and it shattered all over the floor.

"Oops." She started to giggle, was worse than his stupid friends when they got drunk. More clumsy and argumentative and harder to handle.

He grabbed her hard, afraid she'd step on the glass and fall off those silly high heels and cut herself. "Watch out. You'll cut yourself. How about you sit on the kitchen countertop, and I'll clean up. And then we'll get you home."

"Help me." She held out her arms to him.

He put his hands on her waist and lifted, getting her up there without any problem, and then she grabbed on to him and didn't want to let go.

"You are absolutely adorable," she said, her hand fiddling with his hair.

Jake closed his eyes and reminded himself she was old enough to be his mother, and that she was Andie's mother and very drunk, and tried not to look at her legs, because he was a guy and female legs of almost any kind just seemed to take over his brain at times, and this could not be one of those times.

He had to get her out of here.

"Hey," he said, figuring out how. "I need to call Phillip. Do you have a phone?"

She pulled her phone out of her tight, tight skirt and handed it to him.

He flipped through her contact list to the name Andie and dialed.

Andie answered. "Mom! Where are you? I've been looking everywhere. Are you all right?"

"She's at my house," Jake said.

Complete silence greeted him at first, and then very softly Andie said, "What?"

"It's Jake Elliott. That's what I was trying to tell you before. Your mother's at my house. She seems to think someone named Phillip lives here, and I can't make her understand she's in the wrong place. I think she's been drinking." Jake waited. More silence. Then added, "Sorry. I thought maybe she'd listen to you. I didn't know what else to do."

He heard Andie muttering to herself for a moment, and then she talked into the phone again. "I'll be right there. Just don't let her leave."

"Okay," Jake said.

And then she hung up.

He looked back at Mrs. Graham, who was grinning broadly at him and playing with her blouse. And he thought about how worried Andie sounded when she thought her mother was calling, remembered the times before she'd been looking for her mother here.

Andie had seemed too perfect to him, with her perfect hair, perfect teeth, perfect clothes, perfect body, perfect everything, and now…he wondered if she had an alcoholic for a mother who sometimes left home and couldn't find her way back.

Andie burst into his house a moment later and the look on her face when she saw the mess and her mother—commenting

on Jake's nice muscles, then playing with his hair some more—
was just awful.

She took her mother by the hand and urged her down.
"Come on, Mom. We have to go home right now."

Her mother teetered on her own two feet. "Where is Phillip?"

Andie shot Jake a puzzled look. "I thought, all this time, she
was with your uncle."

All this time?

Jake shrugged, didn't know what to say.

"Phillip? It must be…oh, no," Andie said. "Phillip Wrenchler.
He lives in the house behind yours. Maybe she's been sneaking
through your backyard and into his. Mom, he's married."

Her mother was looking at Jake. She winked at him.

Andie rolled her eyes and swore, then looked at Jake pleadingly. "I don't suppose…if I begged you. Absolutely begged
you. You could promise not to tell anyone about this."

"Okay," Jake said.

"Not anyone," Andie said.

"Promise. Want me to help you get her home?"

"No. She'll come with me now. I'm sorry. About the mess
and everything."

Jake shrugged. "It's all right. I'll clean it up. No problem.
Sorry about…your mom."

Andie looked for a moment like she was about to cry, then
took her mother by the hand and led her out of there.

He was still cleaning up the mess when his uncle got home.

Nick caught himself whistling as he walked from Lily's
house to his.

Whistling.

Some kind of song…he couldn't remember who sang it or
much of the lyrics. Something about an absolutely beautiful
day…waiting and waiting and at last experiencing an absolutely perfect day.

The woman did the oddest things to him.

And the absolute best things.

He ran a hand across his jaw, felt the abrasive stubble there and remembered the slightly reddish tint to Lily's cheeks and her pretty lips. If they kept this up, he'd have to start hiding a spare razor somewhere over there, so he didn't scruff her up.

She was so soft.

He didn't want to hurt her in any way.

As it was, it was all he could do to drag himself out of her bed and out the door before her girls got home, and he lay in his bed at night alone waiting for the hours to go by until they could be alone again.

He got to his door, pulled it open, walked into the kitchen, and found that the place reeked of alcohol, and there stood Jake with a broom, trying to clean up broken glass.

Well, hell.

Jake froze, broom and a dustpan full of glass in hand, the garbage can sitting to the side of the kitchen. He'd obviously been at work for a while.

"Hi," he said, looking worried.

"Jake." Nick tried not to bellow. "What's going on here?"

"Okay. It's not what it looks like. I promise."

"Really?"

"Yeah. I can explain." Jake dumped the glass into the garbage and then stood there, looking more worried with every passing minute. "I mean, I would, if I could."

"Oh, you're going to explain," Nick said, taking the broom and the dustpan from his hands, putting them down and pulling Jake along with him, out of the mess and into the living room. "Sit."

Jake didn't. He stood there. "I mean, I kind of promised I wouldn't tell. But…it wasn't me. I wasn't drinking, I swear."

Nick tugged on the kid's shirt, which was wet, sniffed, then rolled his eyes. "You reek of Scotch."

"I know, but I didn't drink any. I was trying to get it away from her—"

"Her? You had a girl over here drinking?" Nick took that like a kick in the gut. The kid was drinking, and he had a girl over, who was also drinking, while Nick wasn't even home? "What the hell else have you been doing while I wasn't here?"

"Nothing. I told you. I didn't do anything except try to stop her—"

"Oh. Okay. You didn't drink anything, you just smell like you did, but you invited a girl over here who was drinking, and you were just trying to stop her? That's your story?"

"No," Jake said.

"Okay, now we're getting somewhere—"

"I didn't invite a girl over. She just showed up."

Nick swore, wanting to grab the kid and scare him into telling Nick the truth. Because the stuff Nick was imagining on his own was pretty bad. The truth could be even worse.

Had Nick missed this completely? That Jake was drinking? That he had a girl? That he had her here, and they were both drinking and doing God-knows-what behind Nick's back?

Had he really missed all that?

"One more time," Nick said, up in the kid's face, letting the fear show and hoping it looked like he was just royally pissed. *Scared straight, Jake. Come on,* Nick thought. "There was a girl here—"

"Well, not really a girl," Jake claimed.

Nick let go of him and backed up, not believing the crap coming out of the kid's mouth. "Not really a girl? What was she, a half girl, half… I don't even want to know what?"

"No, I mean, it wasn't another kid. It wasn't somebody my age."

"You're trying to tell me you're seeing someone old enough to drink?"

"No! You don't get it at all!" Jake yelled, looking like he was about to cry all of a sudden. "I thought you trusted me! I thought we were doing okay. I thought everything was going to be okay!"

"So did I," Nick roared back. "Now tell me, what the hell did you do?"

"I got drunk!" Jake screamed. "That's what you want to believe, fine. I got drunk. I was trying to clean up the mess before you got home, and you caught me. End of story."

Then he stalked off toward the door, like that was it. Like Nick would just let it go with that.

"Oh, no." Nick grabbed him by his arm. No way he was letting the kid leave.

Jake jerked away from him, stronger than Nick expected, and then he had to grab for him again. Next thing he knew they were scuffling, him trying to get some kind of hold on Jake, and Jake squirming and somehow slipping away.

"I swear to God, Jake, if you don't get your ass back here and tell me—

"I already told you," Jake yelled. "It didn't do any good the first time, and I'm sure not going to tell you again. Just let me go."

Nick was trying not to hurt him. He was mad as hell and scared and determined not to let him go, but not to hurt him, either, and it was the Scotch on the floor and the glass that did him in.

Jake got through it, or maybe he got around it, and Nick didn't, skidded on it and lost his footing and went down hard as Jake shot out the door.

Nick laid there and swore some more.

Chapter Thirteen

When he got himself up off the floor, he peeled off his shirt, which smelled as bad as Jake's did and then cleaned up the kitchen, taking the time to try to calm himself down.

Then he grabbed his phone and called Jake's cell, fear shooting through him all over again when it rang and rang and then went to voicemail.

"Jake, get your ass back here. Right now," he said, then could have kicked himself for it.

That was a message sure to make the kid come right home.

He called again, forcing some measure of calm into his voice, he hoped. "Look, we'll talk this out, okay? We'll both be calm, and we'll talk this out. You just…you can't run off like that, Jake. You just can't."

Which was stupid of him to say, because the kid had done just that.

The thing was, Nick had worked Missing Persons for the last year and a half. He'd seen a lot of kids take off after some kind of argument and end up in all kinds of trouble. Or worse, never come back home.

So he was probably overreacting here.

Probably.

But he was scared half to death.

Nick pulled out a sheet of paper with names and phone numbers. He made sure to know who the kid hung out with. He tried the top three kids and all of them swore they hadn't seen Jake and didn't know where he was.

And then, more than anything, Nick just wanted Lily.

Hell, maybe the kid had gone there.

He adored Lily, after all.

Nick went tearing over there and pounded on her back door, obviously scaring her from the look on her face when she flung open the door.

"What's wrong?"

"Jake's gone," he said grimly. "We had a nasty fight, and he's gone. I was hoping he might have come here."

"No. I haven't seen him. What did you fight about?"

"Him drinking. I really screwed up, Lily, didn't have any idea. I must have missed it completely, but I went home and the place reeked of alcohol. So did he, and then he tried to tell me it was all a big misunderstanding and got mad at me for not believing him. Then he took off."

"Okay." She put her hands on his arms, like he might need her to hold him up or something. "Just...take a breath. Teenagers can be really dramatic at times. Believe me, I've heard it all from Marcy. He just probably needs some time to cool down, and then he'll be home, and you two can figure this out."

"What if he doesn't come back?" Nick said, giving voice to his greatest fear.

"Of course, he'll come back. He's not stupid, just mad."

Nick stood there, chest heaving as he fought for breath, fought to calm down. Lily smiled up at him, like he was being ridiculous, and then wrapped her arms around him and just held him.

Which he would have said was silly and completely unnecessary, for him to actually need someone to comfort him. But he all but crushed her to him, afraid he might squeeze the breath right out of her, feeling like he needed her so much right then it terrified him almost as much as the idea that Jake was out there somewhere, alone, and might never make it back in one piece.

"Oh, my God, Lily!"

"It's terrifying, I know. You love your kids so much, like you didn't even know you could love anyone or anything, and then you see that at times you're powerless to keep them safe, and it's absolutely terrifying."

He sagged back against the wall, looking down at her, taking the words in and processing them as fast as he possibly could.

He loved Jake?

Of course he did. Jake was a cool kid, fun to play with when Nick showed up at his sister's house for a weekend here and there. They'd play ball, wrestle sometimes, battle over some silly video game. That was it.

But Lily was saying something different.

Lily was talking *love,* that fierce, you-are-mine, heart-and-soul, and I-would-do-anything-for-you kind of love he'd heard inklings of in the relationship between parent and child, but never thought to experience himself.

Did he love Jake like that?

"Nick, you didn't really think you could do this and not feel that way about Jake in the end, did you?" she asked.

"No. I mean, I didn't really think about it. It all happened so fast, and we were all so shocked that his parents were really gone, and then someone had to be here with them. It's what my sister wanted, so I said we'd try it, and here we are."

Lily nodded, smiled once again, like it all made sense to her. "Welcome to parenthood. It's brutal at times."

"The kid is gone," he said, practically yelling. "He's gone, and I don't know where he is. I don't know what to do—"

Lily put a hand to his mouth, trying to shush him and soothe him at the same time, when all he wanted was to scream.

Did she not understand?

He'd screwed it all up, and the kid was gone!

"I know," Lily said.

"Then tell me what to do now. Tell me how to fix this, because I don't have any idea—"

"Mommy!"

They both heard Ginny at the same time, stopped talking and jerked apart.

Ginny gave them both an odd look, then asked, "Are you guys arguing about Jake?"

"We're not..." Lily stopped, then started again. "We're not arguing. Jake is gone, and his uncle is worried about him. That's all."

"It sounds like you're arguing," Ginny said accusingly.

"Sorry," Nick said. "She's right. I was yelling, and I'm sorry. I'm not mad at your mom. I'm just...scared and sometimes when I get scared, I yell."

Ginny frowned, like she might take him to task for that, but in the end, decided to accept his explanation. "Okay. Just don't do it again. You scared Brittany."

Then she held up the cordless phone and said, "It's Jake."

Nick went to grab it from her, but Ginny put it behind her back and told Nick, "He wants to talk to Mom. He said he can hear you yelling at her, and he wants you to stop right now."

"He can hear me?" Nick asked.

Ginny shook her head, then gave the phone to her mother.

Put in his place by a nine-year-old, Nick stood there, looking out into the darkness. Lily had her kitchen windows open to the night breeze, which meant Jake was either in the house hiding or somewhere in one of their yards.

Which meant, he was safe, wasn't he?

Nick put his hands on the kitchen countertop, bracing himself, and leaned into them, telling himself the kid was safe, crisis averted, and to calm down.

It wasn't working.

He was still terrified.

Lily put down the phone and said, "He's in the tree house. I'm going to go talk to him."

"No. This is my mess. I'll talk to him."

"Nick, trust me on this, okay? You're not ready to fix this, and he doesn't want to talk to you right now. And whatever happened tonight doesn't have to be solved tonight. He's fine. He's safe, and I'll take care of him for now and make sure he doesn't go anywhere except my house or yours, okay?"

"But—"

"I know. You want to charge in there and settle this right now, and I'm telling you that you don't have to. You can let it sit overnight, and you both can calm down and this will all look much better in the morning. I promise."

Nick felt like his entire body was an engine revving at a hundred miles an hour or so, and that charging in to settle things sounded really good to him right now. Essential, even.

And at the same time, he felt like a wet noodle, like there were no bones in his body, no strength, no courage, nothing but a kind of relief that soaked through him and left him weak in its aftermath.

He took a breath, then another, found it just didn't help. He felt like he might fall down at any second.

He'd wanted so much to do this right, for his sister and for Jake, and worried all along that he couldn't, that she'd made a mistake in asking him to, and that he'd end up disappointing her and Jake in the end.

He felt like he'd done all those things tonight.

"Just stay here until I get back, okay?" Lily asked.

"Okay," he finally said, getting out of the way and letting her go.

He watched as she made her way into the backyard and then climbed the ladder into the tree house and disappeared.

He'd imagined the kid hitchhiking to Alaska or someplace like that, and all Jake had done was crawl into the tree house in the backyard next door.

Still, the drinking, the girl, the lying...

How much had he missed? He was afraid to find out.

Nick turned around and found Lily's daughter waiting there staring at him with a mildly disgusted look on her face.

"Grown-ups are so weird," she told him.

"Really?"

Ginny nodded, then took him by the hand. "Come on. You have to talk to Brittany. She liked you so much for building her that stupid tree house, and now you ruined it all by yelling at our mom. You have to say you're sorry and make her think you mean it."

"I do mean it," Nick said.

He had no right to take his temper or his fears out on Lily, and he'd never wanted to scare her girls.

"Just make Brittany believe it," Ginny said, like she might never believe he was sorry, but hoped her sister might.

Jake didn't think he'd ever been so miserable in his entire life, maybe not even the day his parents had their accident.

Because even then, his uncle had called and made it clear that he was on his way, that he would get there as fast as humanly possible, and that he would take care of everything.

And Jake had believed him.

Then he'd found out his parents had made sure that if

anything happened to them, his uncle was to take Jake, and Jake had told himself that it would be hard, but okay, because it was like his parents were still taking care of him, by making sure his uncle was there for Jake.

But now, his parents were gone, and he wasn't going to have his uncle to count on, either.

Which meant, he didn't have anybody who believed him and trusted him and was on his side. Which was the absolute worst feeling in the world.

Then he heard someone climbing the steps to the tree house and thought he might jump off the balcony to keep from having to see his uncle right now, but when he scrambled over to the opening, it was only Lily.

Jake got back in his corner, thankful for the near-darkness, and swiped at tears with the back of his hand and waited in all his misery.

Lily wasn't much like his mom, who said it took a drill sergeant to raise three boys, and she did work hard to keep them in line, tough but fair and lots of fun. Lily was quieter and gentler and really, really sweet.

She climbed into the tree house and sat down beside him, her back to the wall, so she wasn't really looking at him, just there with him, which he liked.

"Sorry he yelled at you," Jake said.

"It's all right. He was just scared."

"He was mad—"

"Yes, but mostly scared," she insisted.

"Well, he didn't have to take it out on you."

"He didn't, Jake. I promise. Now why don't you tell me what happened?"

"He doesn't believe me. That's what happened. I told him the truth, and he doesn't believe it!"

Lily sighed. "Well, you have to admit, it's kind of hard to believe. I mean, he comes into the house. Someone's obviously been drinking. There's alcohol all over the place. It's all over you—"

"You don't believe me, either!" he cried.

"I didn't say that. I'm just saying…try to look at it from his point of view. The situation looks pretty bad."

"He could have believed me," Jake argued. "I don't lie to him. I know he doesn't really want to be here, taking care of me. But we're doing okay. And I've done everything I could to make it easy for him, but then, the first little thing goes wrong, and he just blows up."

"Jake, if he didn't want to be here, he wouldn't be here—"

"Nuh-uh. This wasn't his idea. This was my parents', and they didn't even say anything to him about it ahead of time. They just decided that if anything ever happened to both of them, he'd take me and my brothers. He was as surprised as we were when we found out, and he didn't want to come here and take care of me. But it's what my mother wanted, and it's kind of hard to say no to your dead sister and your dead sister's kid, you know?"

"Okay. Okay." Lily leaned closer to his side and put an arm around his shoulder.

Jake didn't want to want that. He wanted to handle this all by himself because…well, just because.

But he was really glad Lily was there.

"Jake, you have to cut him some slack. Parents don't always know the right thing to do, and with Nick, who's never been a parent before, it's even harder to know what's right when—"

"My mother would have believed me," he insisted.

"Would she really?"

"Yes," he said, then started crying again.

"Oh, Jake. I'm sorry. I'm so sorry."

And then he just gave up and put his head on Lily's shoulder and cried.

* * *

They had something of an armed standoff that night.

Jake refused to go home, and Nick refused to leave without Jake. Lily thought they were two of the most stubborn men she'd ever met, and she finally got tired of trying to broker a deal between them.

She put Brittany to bed in her room, offered Jake Brittany's bed and offered Nick the sofa in the living room.

Ginny thought the whole thing was really funny when Lily explained that Jake wouldn't go home, and Nick wouldn't leave without him, so they were both staying.

Then Ginny said, "Sometimes I don't want to go to Daddy's new house, but you still make me."

And then Lily ended up inviting Ginny to sleep in her bed, too, so they could talk about some daddy things and some divorce things, and when both the girls were finally asleep, and Jake was in Brittany's bed, Lily slipped down the stairs to the living room.

Nick was sitting in the dark, staring at nothing, still as a statue, like a man afraid to move.

Lily curled up in the corner of the couch, just watching him for a moment, aching for him.

"It's kind of scary, being a parent," she said.

"Kind of terrifying, don't you mean?"

She nodded. "Sometimes. But a lot of the time, it's great. And he's fine, Nick. He's upstairs, tucked into a little girl bed with half a dozen stuffed animals watching over him. He's just fine. You both will be fine. You'll see."

"Where would he have gone if you weren't here?" he asked, anguished. "And then what would I have done?"

"It doesn't matter, because I am here and I'm not going anywhere."

"Lily! I don't—"

She was done talking. She put her arms around him and

pulled him to her, leaned back against the big, pillowed end of the couch and stretched out, pulling him down beside her until his head was on her shoulder, his arms wrapped around her. She'd have thought she was asking him to bend steel in his spine, the way he had so much trouble simply accepting that bit of comfort from her.

Was the man so unbending?

"Just close your eyes and tell yourself he's upstairs," she told him. "And he's safe—"

"Your girls—"

"Are asleep in my bed. I'll stay here with you until you fall asleep, and then I'll go up, too."

She leaned down and kissed the top of his head and his forehead and then his lips, just once, then tightened her arms around him and relaxed into the feeling of having a big, strong, for once incredibly vulnerable man in her arms and gave him what comfort she could.

And she tried, she really tried, to tell herself not to fall in love with him. They were just having fun, enjoying each other's company, enjoying being alive.

It wasn't love, but it was enough, Lily told herself.

He didn't even know he loved Jake, when it was so clear to her that he did, and the way Jake told the story, Nick still thought he was only here with Jake out of a sense of duty and obligation. A man like that wouldn't have even given a second thought to loving a woman or maybe even believing he could love her or stay with her.

Lily could have cried herself to sleep, if she'd let herself.

Instead, she'd come down here to comfort him, because for now, he was here and she could have him in her arms and try to make things better for him and Jake.

Tomorrow, she'd try to figure out how to make things better for herself, to protect herself from both of them, if that was even possible anymore.

* * *

Jake stalked back home the next morning, his uncle following behind him. They walked into a kitchen that still smelled like Scotch, and without saying a word, worked together to clean up the mess. Then Jake went upstairs, took a shower and headed off to school.

He wasn't going to say he was sorry for something he didn't do.

He wasn't.

He was halfway to his friend Brian's house to catch a ride to school when a silver BMW stopped beside him. The window came down and there was Andie.

Wow. Never would have believed anything like that would be waiting for him this morning, or that anything could happen that would make him really not care about the mess of the night before.

Life was just full of surprises, and they weren't all bad, he was discovering.

"Want a ride?" she asked.

"Sure," he said, going to the other side and getting in.

She looked like she'd had as tough of a night as he had, and he felt bad about that. Really. "Did you get your mom home okay?" he asked.

She nodded, didn't seem like she wanted to talk about that.

"Nice car," Jake tried. And it really was.

He'd never been in a BMW before, just admired them from afar. The ride was so smooth, and she didn't do anything but barely hit the gas and off it went. The car would probably fly.

Jake couldn't wait to get his permit. Not that his uncle would be eager to let him do that now.

"This is my mom's car," Andie said. "I didn't think she'd be going anywhere today. Or that she should go anywhere today. She probably won't even be awake today until I get home. So I took it."

"I didn't tell anybody about...anything," Jake said. "If that's what you're worried about. And I won't tell anybody. Promise."

She didn't look like she believed him, but he couldn't make her. She'd just have to wait and see, because if he hadn't told his uncle last night, he wasn't going to tell anybody.

"I'm really sorry my mom... I saw the way she was acting with you. She flirts when she drinks too much. It's really disgusting, and sometimes I wish she'd just die and get it over with. I mean... Oh, my God. I'm sorry. I mean... Your parents... I heard... I'm sorry. You must think I'm awful to say that about my mom."

Jake shrugged, trying to play it off.

No big deal.

He had no idea how to handle the topic of his parents' deaths when kids his age brought it up or what to say. It wasn't like there was anything he could really say, after all, to make it better.

"Look, we both have stuff to deal with, and we're dealing, right? I just... You don't have to worry. I'm not going to say anything about your mom. And if you get into a spot again and need somebody to help you with her, you can call me. I won't mind."

Yeah, Jake thought, hoping the next time he helped her out it wouldn't lead to World War III between him and his uncle.

Nick had been watching Jake leave, because he wanted to make sure he was gone before he started searching the house. He figured he had to do that, at least, to see... Well, just to see what else he might have missed.

He'd start in the kitchen and try to remember every drop of liquor he'd brought into the house. The Scotch, he remembered, came from a buddy of his in the marines who lived in town. He'd brought it to Nick's sister's funeral, and they'd had a drink together afterward in his sister's house, and it had ended up in a box of kitchen stuff that Nick had brought here when he and Jake moved in.

So he'd search, find everything that was here and pour it out.

Then he was going to search Jake's room.

He didn't think he had a choice.

He had to know what Jake was doing. He had to keep him safe, as best he could.

Beyond that...

Nick swore long and loud, then glanced out the window and down the street in time to see Jake get into a little silver BMW.

What the hell?

Nick didn't know anybody who drove a car like that.

He didn't think, just reacted. A minute later, he was in his car following them, thinking they could be going anywhere, doing anything, and what would Nick know about it?

A thousand lousy, scary possibilities ran through his head.

But all they did was drive to school.

Jake and a girl, a scarily attractive blonde. It might be the same one who'd been in Jake's room that day.

"Oh, hell," Nick muttered.

No fifteen-year-old boy could think straight around a girl who looked like that.

Nick wondered if she was the one who liked Scotch, if she was the one Jake was covering for, because honestly, he'd probably do anything for a girl like that.

So Nick went home and searched every inch of Jake's room and didn't find much of anything. No drugs. No alcohol. A few condoms and some magazines, but Nick didn't think any fifteen-year-old's room was without those.

He was trying to figure out where to search next when the phone rang.

He grabbed it, hoping in an instant that it was Lily, but all he got was Joan, ready to tell him that he was in no way cut out to be a father to Jake.

Don't I know it, he thought bitterly.

Chapter Fourteen

He did not intend to see Lily that day, thinking it would be best to back off a bit, to think, to make sure he was taking care of things here with Jake, instead of running off to enjoy himself with her.

He was here, after all, to take care of Jake.

Not to fall for a woman.

Not that he'd ever really let himself fall for a woman.

He didn't intend to need her, to depend upon her or to lean on her, and yet he'd done all of those things. And when he sat back and thought about it, it was damned disconcerting to realize how entangled they'd become in each other's lives.

That it had distracted him from seeing obviously troubling things going on with Jake was even worse. He'd never shirked his duty because of a woman. He wouldn't do that now, no matter how much he liked being with her.

Which meant it was better to deal with this now, before they got even more entangled with each other and before he really hurt her. Honestly, he'd never wanted to hurt her.

And it wasn't fair to her, to keep going with this, when…

Well, it just wasn't fair.

Nick leaned into the kitchen doorframe, looking out across their yards, to her kitchen and saw her there, looking back at him.

She knew too much. She saw too much. She wanted more than he wanted to give, and he was sure she knew that, too.

Like anything could ever be simple with a woman like her.

So this was one more thing he'd screwed up and needed to fix.

Grimly, he opened the door and headed for her house. She held her head high and tried to smile, and he felt like a complete jerk, but forced himself to go on, to do this.

"Jake was on the way to school this morning when he got into a car with a girl. A girl with a little silver BMW, looked brand-new. I think it was the same girl who was in our house with him that day. Does Andie Graham have a silver BMW?"

"No," Lily said. "But her mother does."

"Then it was her." *Great.*

"Wait, did they actually go to school?" Lily asked.

"Yeah. I followed them, watched them walk all the way inside. Then I went back to the house and searched his room. I could have taken the place apart without him knowing about it, but then I thought maybe I wanted him to know that I was watching him that closely, so that maybe he wouldn't do anything stupid."

"Did you find anything in his room?"

"No. But that doesn't mean there never was anything there."

"I know, but he seems like a really good kid, Nick. He's almost always at home if he's not at school, and you're almost always there with him. I'm just saying, he doesn't have much of a chance to do anything really bad, does he?"

"Yeah, but if he wanted to find a way, he could. Kids can always find a way, and their parents have no idea what they're really doing or what kind of trouble they're in until it's too late. I've seen it, Lily. I know what the world's like out there."

"No, you know what the worst of it's like. Not what most kids are like," she argued, coming to him, touching him with a hand on his arm, when he'd purposely stayed away, not letting himself touch her. "Maybe you've just seen too many bad things, Nick."

"I know I have," he admitted. "I absolutely know it."

"Look, you should know Jake's convinced you don't really want to be his guardian, that you're going to try it for a few months, but that in the end, you'll go back to your old life and he'll go to someone else. It may have just been that he was upset last night, but that's what he said, and I thought you should know."

Nick nodded, trying to remember exactly what he'd said in front of the kid and what he hadn't. It had just been such a shock. His sister dying. Her husband dying. Them wanting him to take Jake.

He thought in the end, he'd just said, *We'll give it six months and see how it goes.*

Sounded reasonable to him, but he could see now it wouldn't exactly be reassuring to a fifteen-year-old boy who didn't know where he'd go next if things didn't go well between him and Nick.

He tried to remember exactly what he'd offered Lily, too, and didn't remember much more than saying he wanted her, and could he just sneak over here to see her when her girls and Jake weren't around.

Not much to offer a woman, either, and yet that's what he'd done.

"I'm sorry, Lily," he said, kicking himself for hurting her, too.

And he didn't really have to say more than that.

She knew.

"It's last night, isn't it?" she asked.

"Last night, I realized Jake was in trouble, and that I'd missed it. I missed it completely, probably because I'd gotten too caught up in you, and it was nice, Lily. It was really nice between us, but it's not why I came here. I came here to take care of him, and I'm blowing it, and that has to stop."

"Right," she said. "It's not that you got really scared when you realized how much you love him, how you might lose him, too. And it's not that you realized you'd gotten used to having him in your life, when you've never really done that before. And it's not that when you were really scared last night, instead of being alone and having to handle it all on your own, you came to me. You wanted me. You even, for a little while on the couch late last night, let yourself need me, and that's just not something you're willing to let yourself do."

He just stared at her. "I said it was good, okay? It was really good, but you knew it wasn't going to last. It's why you didn't want to get involved with me in the first place, remember?"

She nodded, tears in her eyes but not falling, chin up, still fighting with that quiet, rock-solid strength of hers that he admired so much. "You're just scared, Nick. That's all."

But it was more than that.

It was him, the way he'd always been, the way he always would be.

"I really am sorry," he said again.

She nodded. "Fine."

"Lily—"

"But I hope you know, it's not going to be this easy for you to walk away from Jake as it is for you to walk away from me."

To which Nick said nothing.

He felt sick just thinking about it and what he'd already done.

Jake came home and found that his room had been searched. Thoroughly. Fuming, he went downstairs to find his uncle, who was in the garage doing something under the hood of his car.

"Find what you were looking for?" Jake growled.

"You know I didn't," his uncle said, standing up to face him.

Jake would have slugged him right there if he hadn't known he'd get his ass kicked. Still, it was tempting.

"So, are you satisfied that I'm not doing anything? Or is this the way it's going to be from now on?" Jake thought about what he'd said, then felt even worse, even more furious. "No, not from now on. Until you leave?"

"Jake—"

"Is this what it's going to be like? I just want to know. It's my life, after all."

"Tell me what really happened yesterday." His uncle tried.

"I did. And you didn't believe me. You still don't believe me, even though you searched my room and didn't find anything. So just…believe whatever you want. I don't care anymore."

And then he stalked off to his room and slammed the door behind him.

Lily worked like a fiend the next few days, lonelier than she'd ever been, heartsick really.

Damned, stubborn man.

Mr. I-Don't-Need-Anybody-and-I-Never-Will.

She ripped old carpet out of Brittany's room, pulling and tearing and generally making a huge mess, taking out at least some of her frustrations through her work. Brittany would not be happy, and neither would Ginny, because they'd be rooming together for a while, as Lily redid the wooden floors in their rooms and painted, maybe installed new light fixtures.

Basically ripping out everything she could, just for the satisfaction of it.

"Stupid man!" she muttered, kicking a rolled up strip of carpet downstairs, watching it land with a satisfying thud at the bottom, then heading back to the bedroom for more. "Stupid, stupid man!"

The next time she kicked a piece of carpet down the stairs, she almost hit Jake, who was standing in her living room.

"Was that aimed at me?" he asked.

"No. Sorry. I didn't know you were there."

"I knocked, but…I think you were yelling and didn't hear me," he said, looking really unsure of his welcome.

"I'm taking my frustrations out on carpet. Want to help?"

"Sure," he said, climbing over the mess she'd made and heading up the stairs.

Lily put him on the other end of the room gave him a hammer, to get up the strips of tacks holding the carpet in place, then thought of something. "Shouldn't you be in school right now?"

"Yeah," he admitted, shrugging like he didn't have a good explanation, just hoped she'd understand.

"Your uncle won't like this," she warned.

"So?"

Lily gave him a look that she hoped said his attitude was completely unproductive and didn't show how much she sympathized with him in having to deal with his stubborn uncle.

"Everybody makes mistakes, Jake. You can't just give up on him," she reasoned, because no matter what went on with her and Nick, Jake was his and Jake needed him.

"Why not? He gave up on me and you both."

So, he knew. Lily had worried that he did and wondered what he'd think of that. "Well, I haven't given up on either one of you," she claimed.

She was hurt. She was lonely, and she was good and mad, and maybe she was a fool, too, but she hadn't given up.

She still thought the man would come to his senses and realize he could have a life here, a really good life.

Whether it was the life he wanted… That was another story.

"Do you think he was really happy before? When it was just him and that job of his?" Lily asked, tugging with all her might on another piece of carpet.

"I don't know. I never really thought about it," Jake admitted.

"I mean, he kept doing it. Why would he keep doing it, if he didn't like it?"

"Because…he didn't know what else to do? Because he didn't know his life could be different, and that he could find another life that he liked better than the one he had."

A woman had to hope, didn't she?

He'd certainly seemed…content, at least, with her.

Of course, he could have just liked having someone next door for regular, no-strings sex and a home-cooked meal every now and then, while he was biding his time here with Jake for another couple of months.

Was he really like that?

Had Lily completely misread him?

She didn't think so.

But she was scared and sad and so lonely she ached.

"I thought this would have to be really boring compared to what he's always done," Jake said. "I mean, he's been all over the world. He used to send me and my brothers and my mother the coolest presents, and the postmarks were from some of the wildest places. I always thought he was the greatest."

Still, he could have been lonely, Lily told herself.

He could be sick of it all, if he'd just let himself admit it.

Was that too much to ask of the man?

"Grab that roll of carpet, and I'll take your scraps, and we'll load up my car and throw it away later," Lily said, and off they went downstairs and into the open garage.

"I'm sorry he was such a jerk to you," Jake said, stuffing the carpet into the back of her SUV while Lily held the back end open. "I'd beat him up for you, if I could, but—"

Lily laughed and gave him a quick hug when he was done. "My hero. That's sweet."

Jake blushed, rolled his eyes and then looked as lost and sad as Lily felt.

"I was thinking," Jake said. "Once my uncle's gone, that…

I might be able to stay here? I could help you out with the house, and I could stay with the girls if you needed to go out. I wouldn't be any trouble, I swear—"

"Oh, Jake," Lily said, ruffling his hair.

"No?" He looked panicked at that.

"No. I mean, I'm not saying no. I'm saying…it's complicated. Your parents named your uncle as your guardian, and you can't just pick someone else and move in with them. It doesn't work like that," she tried to explain.

"But he doesn't want me—"

"You don't know that. You just had a fight, that's all. Teenagers and their parents and their guardians fight. It happens. Surely you had fights with your mom and dad?"

"Yeah, but they would have never given up on me," he said, then got all choked up. "Of course, I didn't think they'd ever leave me, either."

"Oh, Jake." Lily wrapped her arms around him and held on while he sobbed.

Poor baby.

She looked up and saw Nick standing by the front door of his house, watching them, his expression looking as hard as something carved out of rock, like it might crack if he showed the least bit of emotion.

Damned, stubborn, stupid man!

"Jake, we will figure this out. I promise. And you are always going to have someone who loves you and will take care of you. That's the most important thing you have to know. You will never be all alone in this world."

But he sobbed like a kid who was facing just that.

Being absolutely all alone in the world.

Jake felt like such a baby, crying in front of Lily, asking if he could come live with her. *God!* Even worse was thinking she might have taken him in that way. He'd thought she really cared about him, that he could count on her, even if neither one of them could count on his uncle.

Stalking back toward the house, he thought if he had to one day, he could go to his brothers' at college. They'd put him up for a while. And then…he just didn't know.

His Aunt Joan's wouldn't kill him, he supposed. He could make her leave him alone, if he really tried. Or at least, push her away. He could be really good at that, it seemed.

Jake walked in the kitchen door, and there was his uncle, on the phone, saying, "I can't make him talk to you, Joan."

Because Jake had been avoiding her very successfully for the past few weeks. Disgusted with them all, Jake held out his hand for the phone.

"You don't have to," his uncle mouthed to him.

Jake grabbed the receiver and took it, liked how it pissed his uncle off, this newfound need to test him physically. Maybe he wasn't all that much stronger than Jake.

"Aunt Joan," he said, "how are you?"

And all the time he was talking to her, he was glaring at his uncle, knowing he couldn't make any kind of fuss about the way Jake had snatched the phone from his hand while he was talking to his aunt.

Jake listened to her for a few minutes, then finally escaped by saying he had homework to do.

He laid the phone down, intending to disappear into his room for hours, but his uncle stopped him by grabbing him by one arm and turning him around.

"Does everything have to be a battle now, Jake?" his uncle asked, right up in his face, seeming massive and just over-whelming.

He'd been an absolute bear ever since he'd broken off with Lily.

Jake shrugged, a little intimidated, but still mad. "Doesn't matter to me."

"Well, I really don't like it. Could we just stop? Couldn't

things go back to the way they were? We were doing okay, weren't we?"

"Back when I thought you trusted me. When I thought you were staying," Jake shot back at him.

"Hey, I'm right here," Nick said. "I haven't gone anywhere."

"You just walked away from Lily. You just turned your back and walked away. How could you do that to her? She's beautiful, and she's really special. I mean, I know I don't know a lot about women, but Lily…" To Jake, that said it all. That his uncle could leave Lily. Jake rolled his eyes and swore. "Do you really think there's anything out there in the world that could be better for you than her? Anyone who'd be better to you? I mean, you almost seemed human these last few weeks. And you almost seemed happy. But if you can't even stay here for her, there's no way you'll stay for me."

"Jake, we're talking about you and me. Not me and Lily—"

"We're talking about your life," Jake yelled back at him. "What do you do out there in the world that's so damned great? Are you always looking for something that's going to be better? Something more exciting, more dangerous, just something… I don't know. More? I mean, what do you think there is, waiting for you out there that you haven't already seen or tried or had?"

"You and me, Jake. Let's talk about you and me—"

"It's one thing not to want to be saddled with a teenager you never wanted, but you could have her. You could have a life here. Her girls are still little. They still need a father, and they're silly and they giggle a lot and they talk way too much. But they're fun to be around, and it's really easy to make them happy. They liked you a lot until you yelled at their mom that night we had a fight. You could have all of that, and you're just going to walk away. I'll never understand that, but honestly, I wish you'd just go ahead and do it. And we can get on with our lives without you."

"That's what you want?" Nick asked him. "You want me to go?"

"I never thought you'd stay," Jake admitted.

He'd hoped he was wrong, but deep down, he'd never really believed it.

He'd been waiting for this day to come.

Nick looked like somebody had kicked him in the gut, like he just hurt.

"We're not done," he called out as Jake stalked out of the room. "Jake!"

But Jake just kept on going.

He went to his room and slammed the door, emptied his backpack of all his school books, just dumping everything on the floor, and started stuffing some clothes into it. Another pair of jeans, a handful of T-shirts, some underwear, some socks.

He wasn't sure where he was going, but he was going.

He'd wait until it got dark, until his uncle went to bed, and then he'd go.

Jake had fallen asleep waiting for it to get dark when his phone woke him. He grabbed it and groggily said, "Hello."

"Jake? It's Andie."

He sat up, wondering if he was dreaming, hoping he wasn't. "Hi. What's up?"

"I'm really sorry about this," she said, and she was crying. Crying really hard. "I just didn't know who to else call."

"What's wrong?" he asked.

"I need help. I really need your help. Can you come and get me?"

Chapter Fifteen

Nick wasn't sure what woke him.

A sound, a feeling, instincts honed over the years.

Something wasn't right.

The clock read 2:43 a.m.

He waited, giving his eyes time to adjust to the dim light, then reached for the locked box he kept under the bed and keyed in the code to open it.

Gun in hand, he heard what sounded like a car door closing, then an engine.

His first thought was that Jake had snuck out and was now coming back home. Jesus, had he missed that, too?

Drinking and sneaking out?

Nick moved silently to the window, pushed open the blinds and saw a car driving away.

No? Saw his own car drive away?

That couldn't be right.

He took off downstairs, pulling on his jeans as he went, out the door and into the street, watching it go.

Somebody had stolen his car out of his own damned driveway? Then he had an even worse thought.

Back inside, up the stairs, storming into Jake's room...

It was empty.

Drawers were open, clothes spilling out, the drawers seeming half-empty.

Jake had dumped his schoolbooks on the floor, but his backpack wasn't there.

Neither was Jake.

Minutes later, he'd locked the gun back up, had shoes and a shirt on, had grabbed his phone, tried Jake's cell three times and gotten no answer. He'd looked, but found that the set of keys he used daily was missing.

Then he was standing outside Lily's back door.

He knew Jake wasn't there. He'd watched his car go down the street, after all, but he still had to hope somehow Jake wasn't in it. That he'd gone to Lily's again.

That it could all be this simple.

He dialed her number, heard her soft, sleepy voice say, "Hello?"

"Lily, it's me. Jake's gone again."

"What?"

"Wake up for me, Lily. Jake ran away. He doesn't have a key to your house, does he?"

"No," she said, still sleepy. "He's not in the tree house?"

"I'm going to check. I didn't want to scare you by doing that and having you wake up and see someone in your backyard. Will you check your house? To make sure he didn't sneak in somehow?"

"Okay. Yeah. I will."

He thought again of Jake's accusations.

You just walked away from Lily. How could you do that to her?

Do you really think there's anything out there in the world that could be better for you than her?

And the worst: *I never thought you'd stay.*

Nick climbed up into the tree house.

Nothing.

Dammit!

He went back to Lily's and a moment later, she opened the back door.

Her hair was a tousled mess, and she wasn't wearing anything but a little cotton camisole and her pajama bottoms, and he had to look away, she looked so soft and good and inviting.

"He's not here," she said.

"Do you mind if I look anyway. Just in case?"

"No. Go ahead," she said, stepping back to let him in. "What happened? Did you two have another fight?"

"Yeah." He took off through the house, opening closet doors, checking all the dark corners, hoping against hope.

Lily followed him. "About what?"

"Me walking away from you and him," Nick said, disgusted with himself and the whole world right then.

And terrified.

The kid terrified him.

The idea of Jake getting hurt, doing something stupid, being all alone out there somewhere, left Nick terrified.

"I didn't say anything to him about us," Lily told him.

"I didn't think you did, but the kid's got eyes, Lily. And he really cares about you. He just knew."

They headed upstairs, checking the girls' rooms quietly and then even Lily's.

Nothing.

"What are you going to do now?" Lily asked.

"Wake up his friends and his friends' parents. Or maybe drive by their houses. I need to borrow your car. I'm pretty sure Jake took mine."

"What?"

"I woke up and heard someone pulling out of my driveway. I'm afraid it was Jake."

"Nick, you came to search my house, but you knew Jake took your car?"

He knew how ridiculous that was.

Yeah, he knew.

He'd done it anyway, had kept hoping however irrational it was that Jake would be here.

"I was pretty sure he was the one who took my car. I was hoping I was wrong," he admitted. "I mean…he doesn't even know how to drive. At least, I don't think he does. I didn't teach him. I don't know if anybody taught him. But I'm sorry I woke you up."

"It's all right. Don't worry about that."

"I'm sorry about everything, Lily. Honest to God, I am. I have no idea what I've been doing these last few months. I screwed it all up."

"Hey." She reached for him, pulling him close for a moment, all softness and understanding and a comfort he'd never understand that came in her arms. "You don't need to do that. Not right now. Just concentrate on finding Jake, and call me when you do, because I'm going to worry about him now. I doubt I'll be able to sleep, so I'll watch for him, in case he comes back home."

Nick dropped his head to her shoulder for a moment, trembling and completely unable to hide it, thinking he really didn't deserve this woman or her kindness or understanding, and yet here it was, and he needed it desperately.

He gave her a quick kiss, then backed away. "I have to go."

"Here. Keys." She grabbed them off a hook by the back door and handed them to him. "Go. I'll call you if he shows up here."

Lily couldn't go back to sleep, so she made a pot of hot tea and sat by the window, where she could see if Jake came home.

He didn't.

She finally called her sister at five forty-five—Marcy got up at that insane hour to do aerobics—and asked her to come over so Lily could help Nick look for Jake.

Marcy was there by six-thirty when an exhausted, worried Nick returned with no Jake in sight.

Lily made a pot of coffee for him, a ferociously strong brew that she knew he favored, and made him sit down and drink a cup.

Marcy was glaring at him—she'd guessed what had happened between them and was furious, even if Lily was only supposed to be enjoying herself with him—but fortunately Marcy kept her mouth shut that morning.

"You checked with all of his friends?" Lily asked.

"Everyone I know of. I pulled his last cell phone bill and woke up a lot of people. Called the twins. He hasn't had time to show up at their school yet, but they'll call if he does or if he calls them. I called a friend of a friend with the local police department and asked them to look out for the car. Called a friend of a friend at the FBI office in Richmond. He's not at any of the hospitals within fifty miles, and he hasn't been arrested." Nick sat here shaking his head. "I don't know what else to do. I find missing people for a living, and I can't even find my own nephew."

"What about his old house?" Lily tried. "That makes sense. If he was upset, wouldn't he go there?"

"One of the first places I checked. He wasn't there."

"How long ago?"

"A couple of hours, why?"

"Let's go back," Lily said. "It's his home. It's a place where he was happy, and he felt safe. I mean… Where do you go when you feel absolutely lost?"

Nick shot her a look she couldn't begin to decipher, like she'd torn something open deep inside of him. "For just about all of my adult life, I'd have gone there."

"Come on. I'll go with you. Marcy's going to stay here and get the girls off to school."

"Thank you," he told Marcy.

"You don't deserve it—"

"Marcy, not now!"

"But I like Jake," Marcy told him. "A lot. So go find him."

He drove fast, just shy of recklessness, incredibly focused and controlled. Lily sat beside him, her hand on his knee, not saying anything and trying not to make a sound as he got a little too close to a car or took a turn a little too fast.

"Sorry," he said, when he realized he was scaring her.

"I'm okay."

"Lily, I'm really glad you came with me. Marcy's right, I don't deserve it, but I'm glad you're here," he said without taking his eyes off the road.

"I love Jake. And I'm afraid I helped push him away. He asked me yesterday if he could come live with me and the girls, once you left, and...I didn't tell him no, but I didn't say yes, either. I tried to explain that it wasn't up to me and him. That you were his guardian, and if he wasn't with you... I should have just said yes. I didn't know he was this close to running away. I mean, he was upset, but I didn't think it was this bad. What happened?"

"Nothing. I can't come up with anything that I thought would lead to this. I can't believe I would have missed things so completely, but he's gone and he took some clothes with him, so I must have done something."

"We'll find him," she said, wishing she could make him believe it.

Nick shook his head, took a turn that had the tires screeching. "A lot of kids aren't ever found."

"And don't you do that. Don't start thinking of every bad thing that could happen. I know you know all of those things.

I know you've seen awful things, but you get the worst of it, Nick. You work on the absolute worst cases, so you have no perspective here. You have to know that."

"If he's not home by noon, we'll have an FBI team. I called in some favors," he told her.

"It's not going to come to that."

They swung past another car, missing its bumper by sheer force of will—Nick's—and Lily couldn't look anymore. She closed her eyes until the car finally stopped.

She expected to be in the driveway, but they were at a traffic light instead.

"You're not going to run it?" Because he had done that more than once already.

"Not this one," he said grimly. "It's the one where my sister and her husband died. Their house is right there, on that corner up on the hill."

Lily turned and looked.

The house was in one of those old neighborhoods of stately, soaring bricks with ivy crawling up the walls, entangling the house and seeming to anchor it to its surroundings even more strongly. Houses that looked like they'd been there forever and always would be. So solid, so strong, so sure.

Lily thought Jake must have felt perfectly secure there and everything about the boy he was now told her he'd been well-loved, too. It made her ache to think of him here and how happy he must have been, how much he'd lost.

"Jake's room is the first window on the corner on the second floor. He had a perfect view of that spot," Nick told her. "You can get here without going through that intersection, but everybody goes through it to town, to Jake's school, to his best friend's houses. And all of his friends are starting to drive now. Even if Jake never drove himself through that intersection, he'd get in a car with friends and they'd all go through it. He'd sit there and take it, rather than tell them how much he hated it."

"You did the right thing, to get him away from that," Lily said.

The light changed. Nick drove up the hill and pulled into the driveway.

Lily hoped to see his car there, but it wasn't.

Nick led her to the side entrance by the garage, and when he went to unlock the door, he stopped and looked at her. "It's not locked. It wasn't even pulled shut all the way."

"Is there an alarm?"

Nick nodded, stepped cautiously inside, keeping her behind him, and went to the alarm panel. "It hasn't been tampered with. It's just not set."

"So…he must have been here, right?"

"If he was, why would he leave the door unlocked and not set the alarm?" He kept Lily behind him and called out, "Jake?"

No answer.

He kept her behind him in the cool, dark house, going room-to-room downstairs, finding no sign of a break-in, but no sign of Jake, either, until they got to the family room.

"Feel that? It's warmer than the rest of the house." He went to the fireplace and stuck out a hand. "Gas logs. They're still on."

Lily saw a pile of afghans on the couch and a chair, throw pillows pulled into place like people had been sleeping there.

Did that mean Jake wasn't alone?

"If he had some kind of party here, I'll kill him myself for scaring us this way," Nick said, his voice absolutely calm for once.

"I'd help you," Lily agreed. "But if that's all it was, why not just tell you he's spending the night with a friend and have you drive him or have one of his friends come pick him up? Much less chance of getting caught that way. For him to steal your car in the middle of the night…something had to happen."

"I'm going to search the upstairs. I'll be right back."

Lily wandered around the downstairs, feeling like an intruder into these people's lives. Like Jake's parents should be walking in the door at any moment.

Because everything was still in place, like they might just walk back in.

So much loss, she thought. So much life, just gone.

Nick came back, obviously having found nothing. "I don't know what else to do."

She took his hand and tugged, leading him back to the family room where it was warmer. Nick sank down into a big, comfy chair next to the fire, looking like a man with the weight of the world on his shoulders.

Lily walked over to stand behind the chair he was sitting in, wanting to comfort him and not knowing what to do, what he'd allow or accept from her.

"It seems like this was such a happy place," she tried.

"It was," he agreed. "And I can't believe the family's just gone. I mean, the boys are still here, but everything's changed. You think those things should be forever, that someone should get forever and get it right and be happy and safe, and I always thought if anybody could have that, it was them. But if they don't even get that kind of happiness...it makes me think nobody ever really does."

Lily put her hand on his shoulder, wanting to do more.

He leaned his head against the back of the chair, and she leaned over the back of his chair and cupped her hand against one side of his face, her cheek against the other. His hand came up and tangled in her hair, holding her there, her tears falling from her face and onto his.

"You should have had this, too," he said. "This kind of happiness...it should have been yours, Lily."

"But not yours?" she asked, her face buried against his shoulder, as he turned his head and kissed her softly on the cheek.

"No. I just never saw that for me. I never believed it could really happen."

"And now you think you were right? That this proves you right?"

"Come here," he said, drawing her around the side of the chair and pulling her onto his lap, wrapping his arms around her and taking a long, shuddering breath.

Lily fought against it, because she had a point to make and intended to make it. "It doesn't prove you were right. Not at all."

"Fine. Tell me everything I'm wrong about, just let me hold you while you do it."

She sank against him, because that's what she really wanted anyway, and because she was cold and tired and so scared, and he was... She sighed, pressing her face to his chest, draped over him like a blanket, thinking this was where she should have been all night, this close to him, facing this together. That they could have gone through this with each other, trusting, knowing, drawing strength from each other.

This was the way life was supposed to be, having someone beside you when things got really rough.

Which was much more than she could try to tell him right now, not when they still didn't know where Jake was.

"You're going to find Jake," she said. "And he's going to be fine, and he's still going to need a home. He wants that home to be with you."

"Not anymore."

"No. This is just a blip. This is regular teenage stuff. You wait. He'll have some explanation that will drive you crazy, but you'll be so relieved that he's home and safe that you won't know whether to yell at him or just collapse right where you are and try to breathe for the first time in hours. And he'll say something and give you one of those goofy grins of his, and you'll think, He's just a kid. A big, overgrown boy who doesn't have half the sense he needs yet to survive in the world, but he's great, and he's yours. He's a great kid."

He sighed. "Lily, this great kid asked if he could come live with you instead of me, not twelve hours ago."

"The only reason he wanted me was because he was afraid

he didn't have you anymore. But he does, and you're going to tell him that as soon as we find him. Now think. Where else can we look? Who can we call? Someone has to know something."

He put his hand in her hair and nuzzled his face against hers and started running through a list of people he'd already called when Lily's phone rang in the distance.

"It's mine." She was praying it was Jake, but it turned out to be Marcy.

"Any news?" Marcy asked.

"No." Lily wanted to scream. She'd thought this was it, that they'd found him.

"Well, I don't know if this has anything to do with Jake, but you've had three phone calls this morning from neighbors asking if you've heard the latest about Audrey Graham. Something about her getting into a fight last night at a party with another woman from the neighborhood for sleeping with the woman's husband. I wouldn't have mentioned it, but someone said her poor daughter saw the whole thing, and didn't you tell me Jake had a thing for Audrey's daughter?"

"Yes, he does," Lily said.

Could Jake be caught up in something with Andie Graham?

Lily turned to Nick. "Did you try to call Andie Graham last night?"

"Yeah. No answer. I even drove by the house. It didn't look like anyone was home. Why?"

Lily shook her head. "Something about Audrey getting in a fight at a party last night and sleeping with one of our married neighbors. Just…wait a minute. Marcy? Which party? The fund-raiser for the heart association?"

"Yes, that was it. Phoenix Rising? Something like that?"

"The Phoenix Club. Okay. Thanks. We'll check it out." She clicked off the phone, then turned to Nick. "Andie's mother went to the heart association ball last night and got into a fight with a woman whose husband Audrey was apparently sleeping with, and it was this big, huge scene, and Andie was there to see it. Do you think, if Andie had a problem, she might call Jake for help?"

"I don't know. He's only fifteen. Why would she call him? Someone who'd have to steal a car to go pick her up?"

"Maybe she didn't know he'd have to steal it. Or that he wasn't licensed to drive it. I don't know. It's something, and it's better than thinking he ran away."

"You know where they live?"

"Yes. Let's go."

They headed out the door and found a police car pulling into the driveway behind them.

Lily felt all the breath go out of her at his stern expression, felt Nick tense beside her as they stopped where they were.

The officer got out of his patrol car, walked up to them and asked, "Everything all right here, folks?"

Nick explained who he was, even pulled out his FBI shield. He told the officer what they were doing, then explained that he was the one who'd asked the local police to keep an eye on the house that morning. "That is why you're here, isn't it?"

"No. Actually, I was following up on a 911 call."

Lily gasped, grabbed for Nick, finding his arm. It was rigid.

"What 911 call?" he asked.

"Possible alcohol poisoning, someone having trouble breathing, maybe needing an ambulance. The operator was trying to get all the information she needed, but the connection wasn't good and before she could get it straight, the caller said not to bother with the ambulance, that they'd transport the victim themselves. We try to follow up on those calls, to make sure we don't have someone in trouble who can't call for help."

"When did the call come in?" Nick asked.

"About forty minutes ago. I would have been here sooner, but I got redirected on a burglary call five blocks away. So, no one's in the house?"

"No," Nick said. "Who made the call?"

The officer flipped through his notes. "Didn't give a name, but it was a female. Gave her phone number as 555-6685. You think the call was about your nephew?"

Nick nodded. "We think he was here. What hospital were they taken to?"

"Get in. We'll use my siren," the officer offered. "I don't think you need to be driving right now."

They sat in the back, side-by-side, his hand clamped down on hers, not saying anything until they came upon a traffic accident being cleared from the road beside them, a familiar-looking black sedan with its side resting against a telephone pole.

Nick went absolutely white. "I think that's my car."

The officer met their eyes in the mirror, reaching for his radio. "Hang on." He asked for information on the accident they'd just passed and relayed it to them. "Black Ford registered to…Nicholas Malone, D.C. plates."

Nick nodded.

The officer went back to the radio to get the condition of the passengers. "The kids seemed good," the officer said. "Conscious, oriented to time and place. The woman was really out of it, though."

"Woman?" Lily asked.

"You have names?" the officer spoke into his radio. "Jacob Elliott, Andie Graham and Audrey Graham."

"Okay. That's them. Thank you," Lily said, squeezing Nick's arm. "We found them."

Chapter Sixteen

Nick had made this ride before, as the agent who helped find the missing.

And by the time he took parents to their missing child, he almost always had some details on the child's condition to relay to the parents. But no matter how reassuring the information was, the parents never really relaxed until they had that child in their arms.

Nick understood that exactly at the moment.

He wouldn't believe Jake was safe until he could see Jake with his own two eyes. He knew he was on his way to Jake and that Lily was beside him, keeping him sane, but nothing else really registered for him. It was like someone had blocked out the world.

He needed this kid like he needed air to breathe, and he needed the woman beside him to stay beside him, to hang on to him, to believe in him, to forgive him, to trust him and more than anything to love him.

"Breathe," Lily told him, hanging on tight.

And maybe to tell him to breathe, too.

The world moved in a surreal kind of drunken fast-forward then, confusing, noisy, crowded. He couldn't make sense of it, but then he was walking down a corridor, and then into a room with cubicles curtained off into tiny spaces for each patient, and then, there was Jake.

Lying on a bed, blood and a nasty looking bump on his forehead, bruised cheek, split lip, looking like he had no idea what kind of reception he was about to receive.

"I kind of messed up your car," he said.

Lily started crying.

Nick just grabbed him and hung on tight.

"So, this was all about a girl?" Nick asked incredulously, finally able to get some answers once the doctor had retrieved the CAT scan results and confirmed that Jake's head injury wasn't serious.

"Not just a girl. Andie," Jake claimed, as if that made all the difference.

Nick turned to Lily, who was still by his side, his eyes pleading, *Help me here.*

Lily fought a grin, knowing how horrifying the night had been. "Jake, what happened with Andie?"

"We've kind of…gotten to be friends. And I like her. A lot. You know?"

"I got that part," Nick told him.

"Well, she's been having trouble, and I've been trying to help her." He looked right at Nick. "You said a man watches out for a woman—"

"You are not a man. You are fifteen—"

"You said we'd watch out for Lily. That we weren't going to stand by and let anybody mess with her—"

"Okay. Yes, I did. Go on," Nick said, thinking a vow of silence might be necessary at the moment.

"Well, that's it, really. I was just trying to help her. Some stuff happened. Some really hard stuff—"

"With her mom?" Lily tried.

Jake clammed up. "I promised her I wouldn't tell."

"Okay." Vow of silence was done. "You're in the hospital. You sneaked out of the house in the middle of the night, stole my car, drove it without a license and wrecked it, with two other people in the car. We're beyond any kind of I-promised-I-wouldn't-tell crap. Spill it."

Lily put her hand over his. He could almost feel her telling him to breathe.

"Jake," she said. "This morning I got three phone calls asking me if I'd heard about Andie's mom getting into a scene at a party last night with Phillip Wrenchler's wife, because Audrey's been having an affair with the woman's husband. So if that's part of the secret you're keeping for Andie, it's out."

"Oh," he said.

"Now," Nick ordered once again, though why, he didn't know. The kid didn't follow orders.

"It's not just this Phillip guy," he finally admitted. "Since Andie's parents' divorce became final a few months ago, Andie's mom started drinking. A lot. And sometimes she disappears, and Andie doesn't know where to find her, and she gets scared. I mean, it's pretty scary when someone you love just disappears."

"Yeah, we got that part," Nick said rolling his eyes.

Jake clearly didn't make the connection.

"Go on."

"So, Andie kept showing up at our house, saying she was looking for her mom, and I knew her mom wasn't seeing you. At least, I didn't think she was. I thought you and Lily were... I mean, I was pretty sure you and Lily were—"

"Yeah, me and Lily. Go on."

"Turns out, Andie's mom was seeing a guy who lives in the

house right behind us. She'd walk down our street and then cut through our backyard, so his neighbors wouldn't see. She got confused one day…. Okay, she got really drunk one day on her way to see him and walked into our house instead, looking for the guy. Next thing I knew, she'd poured herself a drink and when I tried to get it away from her, I spilled it all over the kitchen."

Nick turned around and swore at the pale green curtain, rather than Jake, then faced the kid again. "You mean, that whole mess between us was because of Andie's mom? You couldn't just tell me it was Andie's mom?"

"Andie was so embarrassed. I had to call her to come and get her mom, and her mom was like…flirting with me in front of her own daughter and stuff…." Poor Jake turned red, just telling them about it.

Nick still couldn't believe it.

All this worry and upheaval and outright terror?

Over a girl?

"Go on," he said.

"Well, that was it, really. Andie and I just talk sometimes. None of her other friends know how bad it is. But since her father moved out, her mother's been drinking, staying out all night, chasing after men. Andie didn't want people to know, but I'm like a stranger, practically, and we don't hang out with the same people at all. I promised I wouldn't tell anybody what was going on. So she talks to me, and she's just so…awesome."

He was beaming by the end.

The kid probably couldn't even breathe around her, much less think.

Nick turned back to Lily, pleading with a look.

"She's a beautiful girl, Jake," Lily told him. "And I'm glad she had you to help her. But this is really the kind of problems two teenagers can't solve. You could have told us. We'd have tried to help her."

"She didn't want anybody to know," he said again, sounding

so sincere, like that made perfect sense. That he'd do the same thing all over again.

It was all Nick could do not to scream. He was still scared half to death. His heart rate hadn't yet settled down, and his muscles had turned to mush. It was a miracle he was still standing.

He made a face and leaned his head back to stare at the ceiling, like there might be answers for him somewhere up there.

Lily squeezed his hand once again, urging him to hang on.

"Tell us what happened last night, Jake?" she asked.

"Andie called. Her mom was at that stupid party, and she got really drunk and then she got into a fight with Phillip's wife. Andie went to try to get her mom out of there, but then her mom couldn't remember where she parked her car or find her keys. Andie was crying and said she just had to get them both out of there. So she asked me to come and get them."

"And you didn't think to mention to her that you don't drive?"

"I can drive," he claimed.

"Not legally," Nick yelled.

Jake winced, looked hurt and sad and very young.

"Okay, fine. I'm sorry," Nick said. "I'm just still a little bit... God, Jake, were you trying to scare me to death?"

"We thought you'd run away," Lily told him in her softest, most soothing, understanding, motherly voice.

"I wouldn't do that," he claimed, like it wasn't even a possibility.

"You packed a bag of clothes," Nick reminded him.

"Oh, yeah."

Oh, yeah! Nick groaned.

"Okay, I was thinking about it, and I threw some clothes in my backpack, but I wouldn't have really done it," Jake claimed.

"Well, we didn't know that," Nick practically roared. "And when you took off in the middle of the night without saying anything and wouldn't answer your phone—"

"Jake, he heard you leave the house eight hours ago. We've been looking for you ever since, imagining all kinds of awful things."

"Oh. Well, all I did was go pick them up and take them to our old house for a while, to hide," Jake said. "Andie's mom was still a mess, and Andie just wanted to hide from everybody to think about what to do next. And I knew you'd be mad, but I was mad, too, that you didn't trust me about anything. And I couldn't figure out what to say to you, so…I just didn't pick up the phone. That's all."

"That's all?" Nick said, nodding and trying to breathe. "And the 911 call? Because we heard about that, too."

"When Andie and I woke up this morning, she went to try to wake up her mom, but she couldn't. It was like she was barely breathing, and then we got scared and called 911. But they said it was going to be about ten minutes before the ambulance could get there, and we didn't think we could wait that long. So I was going to drive her to the hospital."

"Because you didn't wreck the first time you drove them that night. So why not do it again?" Nick said, admittedly a little too heavy on the sarcasm. He closed his eyes, so he couldn't glare at Jake. "Then what?"

"I'm not really sure. One minute, we were fine, and then I kind of hit the curb and tried to get back in my lane. But I guess I went too far back the other way, and we slid into the telephone poll. Am I in a lot of trouble for that?"

Nick's eyes popped open and he just stared at the kid, dumbfounded.

Am I in a lot of trouble for that?

"Lily," he said again.

She leaned over and gave Jake a big hug, making him look even more like a silly, little kid in serious need of mothering and fathering. "We were just so worried about you."

She soothed him, which Nick supposed the kid needed, while he thought, *Do kids just have no sense at fifteen?*

Could that even be possible, that their reasoning and judgment could be so lacking at this age?

He knew Jake wasn't stupid. He'd seen the kid's report card. Which just meant...

Fifteen?

Could it be this bad? This scary for a parent?

Then he thought about Joan.

Joan would love it when she heard about this. This was the kind of ammunition she'd been waiting for to use against Nick and his guardianship of Jake. She'd be thrilled.

"Excuse me?" a girl's voice asked.

Nick turned, and there she was, Jake's most wondrous girl in the world. Andie Graham, in all her adolescent, leggy, blond glory, plus a few bumps and bruises, but otherwise whole.

Nick wanted to beg her to never come near Jake again, and to explain to Jake just how dangerous women could be.

Look how much trouble this one had caused them both already.

"I just wanted to make sure Jake was okay," she said.

Jake practically glowed with happiness from his hospital gurney, might have even winced a bit as he grinned, whether as a complete play for sympathy or because his head hurt, Nick had no idea.

"I'm fine," Jake said. "Are you okay?"

She nodded, then waited there on the edge of Jake's little space.

"How's your mom, Andie?" Lily asked.

Andie bit her lip for a moment, looking embarrassed, then said, "The doctors say she'll be fine."

"Good." Lily leaned over and gave Jake a hug. "We'll be outside for a few minutes."

Nick didn't intend to go anywhere. He didn't trust this girl alone with Jake for a moment, but Lily took him by the hand

and led him out of the room. They went down the corridor and
around the corner until they'd found a relatively quiet spot.

"You think that was a good idea? Leaving him alone with
her?"

Lily laughed. "What are you going to do? Lock him in his
room for the next six years until he's twenty-one?"

"Can I do that, as his legal guardian? Because it doesn't
sound like a bad idea."

Lily laughed some more and wrapped her arms around him
and just held on tight. Nick couldn't get her close enough. He
sagged against the wall at his back, and then it was like Lily
and the wall were all that kept him on his feet.

Relief washed over him like he'd never felt before, leaving
him weak and exhausted and still terrified somehow.

"Oh, my God, Lily!" he said, his face buried in her hair. "He
wrapped the car around a telephone pole, swerved all over the
road. I don't know how all those other cars missed him. He
could have killed that girl and her mother while he was trying
to save them. He could have killed himself—"

"I know. But he didn't. And he's fine—"

"And stupid! How can he be this stupid? A few surging hormones and adolescent dreams, a pair of long legs on a pretty
girl, and he just turns stupid? Is that the way it works?"

"You never did anything stupid over a girl?" she asked.

"Not like…" He couldn't say that, because it wasn't true.

Nick took a breath and then another one, just couldn't seem
to get enough air in his body to make his head stop spinning.
Then he looked down at her, trying to make it sink in. That the
night was over, and Jake was safe, and they'd all lived through
it, somehow, and Lily was here by his side.

"I was going to say I never had," he told her, a hand tangling
in her hair. "But I had my own pretty, long-legged blonde, and
I thought I could just walk away from her somehow."

She gave him a pretty smile through her tears.

"Tell me you knew all along how stupid that was of me, to think I could really walk away from you. Because I'd hate to think you believed I could and that I'd hurt you that much, Lily."

"I was hoping you couldn't."

"You were right," he told her. "Are you going to forgive me? For ever thinking I could live without you?"

"I don't know," she said, still smiling, a twinkle in her pretty blue eyes. "I mean, how do we know you've really learned your lesson?"

"I cannot raise this kid without you," he said. "I don't want to. I don't want to do anything without you, Lily."

She gave him a kiss, then another.

He pulled back, taking her face in both his hands, all teasing aside. "I think I knew all along, right from the first moment I saw you. I knew you'd be trouble, and I should stay away—"

"Me? Trouble?" She feigned outrage.

He nodded. "But I just couldn't resist. Especially after you helped me get rid of Audrey that day in your kitchen. I could not stop thinking about you. And your neck."

"You're the one who caused all the trouble—"

He laughed, kissed her again. "But when I really knew there was no going back, was when you wanted to go to Jake's house, to look for him again, and you asked me where I would go when I was really scared and sad and feeling all alone in the world. And I realize, the answer is easy for me now. I'd go to you."

She took a breath, started to cry then.

"And everything would start to get better, because you'd be by my side. I need you to always be by my side, Lily. I love you, you know? And I've never said that to another woman in my life, and I promise you, I never will."

"I love you, too," she said, kissing him quickly, urgently, her tears falling fast.

"You can have as much time as you need to be sure and for your girls to get used to me and the idea of us being together, but I want you to promise me now that you'll marry me."

"I will," she promised.

"Just think, we'll actually get to sleep in the same bed all night," he said.

"If you let me sleep." She grinned. "And you have to let me work sometimes, Nick. We have to get some work done."

"We will. Although, afternoons in bed… You have to admit, it's a really nice way to live, as often as we can get away with it."

"You should be warned," she told him. "I've heard teenage girls are so much scarier to raise than teenage boys."

He groaned. "You're kidding."

Lily shook her head. "Too late to back out now."

Lily woke the next morning stretched out on her side, the front of her body chilled, the back all toasty and warm.

Leaning back into that luxurious heat, she felt it give beneath her weight, until she rolled over and found Nick propped up on his side, bare everywhere she could see and most likely where she could not, judging by the feel of his strong, solid length pressed to hers.

He leaned over and kissed her softly, then brushed her hair back from her face, giving her a beautiful smile.

"It's about time I got to wake up with you," he said. "And have you in my bed. I've wanted that for a long time."

Lily smiled back at him, the crazy, scary night they'd spent searching frantically for Jake and the exhaustion of the next day finally over. Marcy had offered to take the girls for the night, and the hospital had kept Jake overnight. Jake, who'd looked highly insulted at the idea that Nick hadn't wanted to leave him alone so soon after fearing Jake had been lost to him for good.

So Nick had brought Lily back to his house, too worn-out

to do anything that night but refuse to part with her. They'd climbed into his bed and slept like the dead, for how many hours she didn't know.

He'd stroked and kissed her awake at some point deep in the night, made love to her urgently, fiercely at first, and then hauled her into his arms and held on to her like she was his only hope of surviving until morning.

That was the last thing she remembered.

Him holding her so tight she could barely breathe, trembling again, her trying to reassure this big, strong, brave man, loving him so much her heart ached with it.

He touched his thumb to her bottom lip, brushing across it, then kissed her again, sweetly, quickly.

"We found Jake," he said, as if he needed to hear it once again.

"Yes, we did."

"And he's safe."

Lily nodded.

His gaze went dark and smoky and serious. "And you've forgiven me for being such an idiot as to think I could ever live without you. As if I'd ever want to."

"Yes," she whispered.

"And you love me?"

"I do. I love you," she promised, reaching up to pull his head down to hers so she could kiss him.

By the time they were done, he'd settled himself on top of her, nudging her thighs apart, his weight on his elbows, back bowed, sliding ever so easily inside her body, still soft and yielding from the last time he'd made love to her, sometime in the night.

She gasped, then gave herself up to what he wanted, needing that connection to him in every way possible, the feelings so intense, still so new. So much had changed so quickly. It was hard to believe any of it was real.

He closed his eyes and groaned, leaning his head down until his forehead touched hers, then started rocking back and forth just a bit, the sensations all the more intense for the slowness with which he moved, the deliberateness, the concentration.

Nick.

She arched into him, trying to make him move faster, harder, deeper.

He kissed the side of her neck, whispered, "Say you're going to marry me. Say it for me now."

As if she'd ever denied him anything.

Lily was trembling. It was as if he'd brought every nerve ending in her body to alert in seconds.

That was what he did to her heart and what he did to her body, and together they were almost too much for any woman to bear. So much more than she'd ever found in any man. A connection she hadn't even known she was missing.

Until she met him.

"Say it," he whispered.

But the words were a pure demand.

"Yes." She gave in. "I will. I'll marry you."

And then the passion he'd held in check, simmering in those exquisitely slow movements of his hips, burst open, in him and in her. She held on tight, felt him surging inside of her, and moments later collapsing in her arms.

When he finally lifted his head and slid to one side to take the bulk of his weight off of her, he looked as vulnerable as she'd ever seen him.

"Tell me you'll never scare me the way Jake did two nights ago. That we can love each other and live together and raise our children together without that kind of terror."

"Oh, Nick. I can't tell you that. No one could."

He nodded, little lines of tension still in his face, put there by the night they'd spent looking for Jake. "I was afraid you'd say that."

"But I can promise that no matter what, I'll be right here beside you, helping you through it."

He kissed her gently, reverently. "I've never had anything in my life that I couldn't stand to lose before. And now...there's just so much. So much I couldn't live without. I love you, Lily. I want to wake up every morning just like this, with you beside me. I want to hold you in my arms every night. I want to give you everything you've ever wanted."

"There's nothing left for you to give," she told him. "Nothing else I need. I've got it all right here, right now."

* * * * *

Want to know what's going on in those suburbs?
Don't miss Audrey's story,
THE NANNY SOLUTION,
on sale in February
from Silhouette Special Edition!

*Celebrate 60 years of pure reading pleasure
with Harlequin® Books!*

*Harlequin Romance® is celebrating by showering you
with DIAMOND BRIDES in February 2009.
Six stories that promise to bring a touch of sparkle
to your life, with diamond proposals and dazzling weddings,
sparkling brides and gorgeous grooms!*

*Enjoy a sneak peek at Caroline Anderson's
TWO LITTLE MIRACLES,
available February 2009
from Harlequin Romance®*

'I'VE FOUND HER.'

Max froze.

It was what he'd been waiting for since June, but now—now he was almost afraid to voice the question. His heart stalling, he leaned slowly back in his chair and scoured the investigator's face for clues. 'Where?' he asked, and his voice sounded rough and unused, like a rusty hinge.

'In Suffolk. She's living in a cottage.'

Living. His heart crashed back to life, and he sucked in a long, slow breath. All these months he'd feared—

'Is she well?'

'Yes, she's well.'

He had to force himself to ask the next question. 'Alone?'

The man paused. 'No. The cottage belongs to a man called John Blake. He's working away at the moment, but he comes and goes.'

God. He felt sick. So sick he hardly registered the next few words, but then gradually they sank in. 'She's got *what?*'

'Babies. Twin girls. They're eight months old.'

'Eight—?' he echoed under his breath. 'They must be his.'

He was thinking out loud, but the P.I. heard and corrected him.

'Apparently not. I gather they're hers. She's been there since

mid-January last year, and they were born during the summer—
June, the woman in the post office thought. She was more than
helpful. I think there's been a certain amount of speculation
about their relationship.'

He'd just bet there had. God, he was going to kill her. Or
Blake. Maybe both of them.

'Of course, looking at the dates, she was presumably
pregnant when she left you, so they could be yours, or she could
have been having an affair with this Blake character before…'

He glared at the unfortunate P.I. 'Just stick to your job. I can
do the math,' he snapped, swallowing the unpalatable possibility that she'd been unfaithful to him before she'd left.
'Where is she? I want the address.'

'It's all in here,' the man said, sliding a large envelope across
the desk to him. 'With my invoice.'

'I'll get it seen to. Thank you.'

'If there's anything else you need, Mr Gallagher, any further
information—'

'I'll be in touch.'

'The woman in the post office told me Blake was away at
the moment, if that helps,' he added quietly, and opened the
door.

Max stared down at the envelope, hardly daring to open it,
but when the door clicked softly shut behind the P.I., he eased
up the flap, tipped it and felt his breath jam in his throat as the
photos spilled out over the desk.

Oh, lord, she looked gorgeous. Different, though. It took him
a moment to recognise her, because she'd grown her hair, and
it was tied back in a ponytail, making her look younger and
somehow freer. The blond highlights were gone, and it was
back to its natural soft golden-brown, with a little curl in the
end of the ponytail that he wanted to thread his finger through
and tug, just gently, to draw her back to him.

Crazy. She'd put on a little weight, but it suited her. She

looked well and happy and beautiful, but oddly, considering how desperate he'd been for news of her for the past year—one year, three weeks and two days, to be exact—it wasn't only Julia who held his attention after the initial shock. It was the babies sitting side by side in a supermarket trolley. Two identical and absolutely beautiful little girls.

* * * * *

When Max Gallagher hires a P.I. to find his estranged wife, Julia, he discovers she's not alone—she has twin baby girls, and they might be his. Now workaholic Max has just two weeks to prove that he can be a wonderful husband and father to the family he wants to treasure.

Look for TWO LITTLE MIRACLES
by Caroline Anderson,
available February 2009
from Harlequin Romance®

CELEBRATE
60 YEARS
OF PURE READING PLEASURE
WITH **HARLEQUIN**®!

**We'll be spotlighting a different series
every month throughout 2009
to celebrate our 60th anniversary.**

Look for Harlequin® Romance in February!

**Harlequin® Romance is celebrating by showering
you with Diamond Brides in February 2009.**

Six stories that promise to bring a touch of sparkle to
your life, with diamond proposals and dazzling weddings,
sparkling brides and gorgeous grooms!

Collect all six books in February 2009,
featuring *Two Little Miracles* by Caroline Anderson.

*Look for the Diamond Brides miniseries
in February 2009!*

www.eHarlequin.com   HRBRIDES09

HARLEQUIN® Romance®

This February the Harlequin® Romance series
will feature six Diamond Brides stories featuring
diamond proposals and gorgeous grooms.

Share your dream wedding proposal and you could WIN!

The most romantic entry will win a diamond
necklace and will inspire a proposal in one of
our upcoming Diamond Grooms books in 2010.

In 100 words or less, tell us the most romantic
way that you dream of being proposed to.

For more information, and to enter
the Diamond Brides Proposal contest, please visit
www.DiamondBridesProposal.com

Or mail your entry to us at:

IN THE U.S.: 3010 Walden Ave., P.O. Box 9069, Buffalo, NY 14269-9069
IN CANADA: 225 Duncan Mill Road, Don Mills, ON M3B 3K9

REQUEST YOUR FREE BOOKS!
2 FREE NOVELS PLUS 2 FREE GIFTS!

SPECIAL EDITION®
Life, Love and Family!

YES! Please send me 2 FREE Silhouette Special Edition® novels and my 2 FREE gifts (gifts are worth about $10). After receiving them, if I don't wish to receive any more books, I can return the shipping statement marked "cancel." If I don't cancel, I will receive 6 brand-new novels every month and be billed just $4.24 per book in the U.S. or $4.99 per book in Canada, plus 25¢ shipping and handling per book and applicable taxes, if any*. That's a savings of at least 15% off the cover price! I understand that accepting the 2 free books and gifts places me under no obligation to buy anything. I can always return a shipment and cancel at any time. Even if I never buy another book from Silhouette, the two free books and gifts are mine to keep forever.

235 SDN EEYU 335 SDN EEY6

Name	(PLEASE PRINT)

Address	Apt. #

City	State/Prov.	Zip/Postal Code

Signature (if under 18, a parent or guardian must sign)

Mail to the Silhouette Reader Service:
IN U.S.A.: P.O. Box 1867, Buffalo, NY 14240-1867
IN CANADA: P.O. Box 609, Fort Erie, Ontario L2A 5X3

Not valid to current subscribers of Silhouette Special Edition books.

Want to try two free books from another line?
Call 1-800-873-8635 or visit www.morefreebooks.com.

* Terms and prices subject to change without notice. N.Y. residents add applicable sales tax. Canadian residents will be charged applicable provincial taxes and GST. Offer not valid in Quebec. This offer is limited to one order per household. All orders subject to approval. Credit or debit balances in a customer's account(s) may be offset by any other outstanding balance owed by or to the customer. Please allow 4 to 6 weeks for delivery. Offer available while quantities last.

Your Privacy: Silhouette is committed to protecting your privacy. Our Privacy Policy is available online at www.eHarlequin.com or upon request from the Reader Service. From time to time we make our lists of customers available to reputable third parties who may have a product or service of interest to you. If you would prefer we not share your name and address, please check here.

SSE08R

COMING NEXT MONTH

#1951 VALENTINE'S FORTUNE—Allison Leigh
Fortunes of Texas: Return to Red Rock
Rescuing the pregnant damsel in distress was all in a day's work for firefighter Darr Fortune. But when he was stranded with sexy, mysterious "Barbara Burton" during a freak Valentine's Day snowstorm, he looked forward to uncovering all her secrets....

#1952 ALWAYS VALENTINE'S DAY—Kristin Hardy
Holiday Hearts
Things were about to get very steamy on this Alaskan cruise, as party girl Larkin Hayes crossed paths with lobbyist-turned-Vermont-dairy-farmer Christopher Trask. Could this unlikely duo make some Valentine's Day magic to last a lifetime?

#1953 THE NANNY SOLUTION—Teresa Hill
Self-made millionaire Simon Collier needed a nanny—for his out-of-control pooch! Audrey Graham fit the bill...and then some. Not only did Simon's five-year-old daughter warm immediately to Audrey, but the live-in dogsitter soon soothed the savage beast of the single dad's lonely heart, too.

#1954 THE TEXAN'S TENNESSEE ROMANCE—Gina Wilkins
After losing her job, attorney Natalie Lofton retreated to her family's Smoky Mountain cabin to nurse her wounds. Then she met handyman Casey Walker. He wasn't very handy—truth be told, Casey was a Dallas lawyer on leave—but he *was* about to prove he could mend hearts with the best of them.

#1955 THEIR SECOND-CHANCE CHILD—Karen Sandler
Fostering Family
Tony Herrara must have been crazy to hire his ex-wife Rebecca Tipton to oversee his vocational bakery and café for adult foster kids! But Becca was best for the job...and his four-year-old daughter fell for Becca instantly. Were Tony and Becca headed down the road to renewed heartache, or was this the second chance they never dreamed possible?

#1956 THE MOMMY MAKEOVER—Kristi Gold
When the little girl bought her widowed mom personal training sessions, sexy health club owner Kieran O'Brien was charmed. Erica Stevens—the mom in question—wasn't. But as Erica warmed to the routine, she discovered that the muscle getting the real workout was her heart—which beat faster whenever Kieran was around....

SSECNMBPA0109